"Well, what do y

Claire stepped up next to Donovan and looked around. "You can see for miles. It's beautiful."

"It certainly is." He pointed to the house. "It's a good view of the house from here."

"You can see how large it is. Much bigger than I thought it was. Are those barns yours?" Claire pointed to three barns to the left of them.

"Yes, they're mine, but they're part of the lease to Mr. Watkins next door."

"You must feel a sense of accomplishment you've got all this at such a young age." Again, she could see why her friend had had a secret crush on him. He was dynamic and, when he wanted to be, charming.

He scoffed. "No, it's never enough."

Claire raised her eyebrows at the concern on his face.

What was it that pushed him to want more when he had so much already?

Samantha Price wrote stories from a young age, but it wasn't until later in life that she took up writing full-time. Formally an artist, she exchanged her paintbrush for the computer and, many bestselling book series later, has never looked back. Samantha is happiest lost in the world of her characters. To learn more about Samantha and her books, visit samanthapriceauthor.com.

THE AMISH MAID'S SWEETHEART

Samantha Price

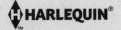

ISBN-13: 978-1-335-49971-4

The Amish Maid's Sweetheart

First published in 2018 by Samantha Price.
This edition published in 2019.

Copyright © 2018 by Samantha Price

Recycling programs
for this product may
not exist in your area.

Printed in U.S.A.

THE AMISH MAID'S SWEETHEART

Chapter One

"I'm sorry, Claire, we simply don't need your services anymore."

Claire's mouth fell open. She blinked hard at Mrs. Wallen, closed her mouth then licked her lips. "Oh."

"It's not that you weren't good. You were marvelous. That's why we took the liberty of recommending you to Mrs. Billings, who runs a B&B."

Claire looked down at her clasped hands and nodded. She knew of Mrs. Billings from her friend Jessie, who had just left her employment. Claire looked up at the elderly Mrs. Wallen. It wasn't her fault her daughter-in-law was insisting on doing the work for her. "Thank you for recommending me."

"My pleasure. I'll miss you. Mrs. Billings said you can go by any time today and see her."

Claire nodded. "I know where Mrs. Billings's bed-and-breakfast is. One of my friends used to work for her."

"Excellent. I am sorry I can't keep you on any longer, but Trudy's insisting she do everything. I think it's too much for her with all she's got to do, but she says she can."

"I understand, Mrs. Wallen, truly I do. It's perfectly all right. I've enjoyed working here even though it was only for a short time. I'll miss you too."

"Goodbye, Claire."

She leaned over and hugged Mrs. Wallen. "Bye."

"Can I call you if things don't work out?"

"Yes. Please do. Our phone's in the barn, but we do have a message service, and I'll call you right back as soon as I'm able."

Mrs. Wallen smiled and nodded.

Claire walked away from the house and took hold of the handlebars of her bike. She didn't want to work for Mrs. Billings. The woman sounded horrid. From what Jessie had said, it wasn't a nice place to work, but neither did she want to stay home all day and work on the farm. Besides, she liked to have her own money rather than be totally dependent on her *familye*.

"Oh, Claire."

Claire was just outside the gate when she heard Mrs. Wallen's voice. She spun around. "Yes, Mrs. Wallen?"

"Douglas said he'd take you to see Mrs. Billings right away if you wish. He's going into town."

"Thank you, but I've got my bike."

"It'll fit in his truck."

"Yes then, thank you. I'll take up the offer."

Douglas, Mrs. Wallen's gardener, was very quiet on the drive to the B&B, but that was typical for him, and that gave Claire time to think. She knew Mrs. Billings was strict and finicky. She also had heard about

Donovan, the son, a dreadful womanizer and not to be trusted. Claire bit her lip. Once again, she told herself jobs weren't easy to come by.

"There you go, Miss," Douglas said, when he stopped outside the B&B. He opened his door, jumped out of the truck and took Claire's bike out of the back.

"Thank you, Douglas."

Douglas nodded a goodbye, and Claire did the same; then he drove away and she wheeled her bike to the side of the building and leaned it against the wall. After a deep breath, she walked to the front and entered the double doors. She had not been inside the place before, but it was familiar thanks to the detailed description she'd gotten from Jessie on their many girlfriends' get-togethers at the coffee shop.

Claire approached the girl behind the desk, who she knew was most likely Yvonne because Jessie had talked about everyone who worked there. "Hello, I'm here to see Mrs. Billings."

The young woman smiled up at her. "Do you have an appointment?"

Claire frowned. "No, I don't think so, but she is expecting me."

"What's your name?"

"Claire Schoneberger."

The receptionist pressed a few buttons on her phone after she directed Claire to have a seat.

"Claire, is it?"

Claire rose to her feet when she saw an attractive, light-haired older woman walking toward her. "Yes, Claire Schoneberger."

"I'm Mrs. Billings. Come this way."

Claire followed the well-dressed Mrs. Billings into a small room to the left of the reception area. She didn't seem as scary as Jessie had said. Perhaps everything Jessie had told them had been an exaggeration.

"Have a seat." Mrs. Billings sat behind a white desk and Claire sat opposite. "You've come highly recommended by some very good friends. I don't mind telling you I've had problems with staff turnover lately. If I give you the job, I would like your personal guarantee you'll stay at least twelve months." Mrs. Billings eyed Claire carefully.

Claire stared into Mrs. Billings's pale brown eyes, searching her head for something to say. Anything could happen in twelve months. Was Mrs. Billings being reasonable to ask such a thing of her? Her upbringing had taught her a verbal promise was binding, as though she'd signed papers. What if she suddenly met the perfect man, got married and the man wanted to move away?

After Claire had taken a while to answer, Mrs. Billings said, "I'm sure you wouldn't be here to waste my time. You wouldn't be here for a job if you only intended to stay a few months; would that be correct, Miss Schoneberger?" Without waiting even a moment for her to reply, Mrs. Billings stood. "Young lady, I take it from your tardy response that you're wasting my time."

"No, wait. Yes, I will stay at least twelve months. As long as you're also happy with my work."

Mrs. Billings smiled and sat back down. She placed thin-rimmed glasses on the end of her nose and looked down at a short stack of papers on her desk. "I pay all my staff quite well, better than the mandated minimum wage." She handed Claire a few sheets of paper as she named a starting wage that raised Claire's eyebrows. Looking down, Claire saw a list of rules and a code of conduct for the staff. "But I also expect a lot. Study those completely. That will save me having to tell you everything. Time is money. I assume you can start tomorrow?"

"Yes, I can start tomorrow." Claire smiled and was pleased to have a job so soon, right away after losing the last one so suddenly.

"Nine sharp. Yvonne will have all the necessary forms for you to fill out. Do that before you leave. Good day, Miss Schoneberger."

Claire stood and nodded. "Good day and thank you."

She hurried out of the office and once she'd filled out two forms giving all her details, she walked out of the building wondering how she would get home. She'd completely forgotten about her bike and decided to walk to the main road to call the *familye* phone from a pay phone.

Just as she stepped onto the side of the road, she heard horse's hooves. She turned to see an Amish buggy leaving the building. Once she squinted hard, she saw it was Olive's *bruder,* Elijah, and his *onkel* Henry. A smile of relief broke out on her face at the realization they'd be able to take her home.

The buggy stopped by her. "Can we take you somewhere, Claire?" Elijah asked her.

"*Jah*, are you going near my *haus*?"

Elijah looked at his *onkel* Henry, who gave a quick nod. "We can take you," Henry said.

Once she was in the buggy, Elijah asked her, "What are you doing out this way?"

"I've just got a job here. I might have gotten Jessie's old job."

Elijah scratched his chin. "I'm pretty sure they've got someone else doing her job."

Claire shrugged. "Jessie said you were doing some building work here."

"That's right. We should be finished tomorrow or the day after. Just watch yourself while you're there, Claire. I didn't want Jessie working there around bad influences."

"I will." Claire knew the bad influences he was talking about came in the form of one man, Donovan Billings, her new employer's son.

"Don't tell Jessie about my new job if you see her today. I want to tell all the girls together. We're meeting late this afternoon at the coffee shop."

"Okay," Elijah agreed. "I won't say a word."

She hoped Jessie would not mind her working at her old job. Hopefully, she'd have some tips for her.

When they were a mile from her *haus,* Claire said, "Just let me out here, *denke.*" Claire wanted to have time to think before she saw her parents. They hadn't been very happy about her first job with *Englischers,* but it was made a little easier because they'd known old Mr. and Mrs. Wallen. They did not know Mrs. Billings and if they learned of Donovan Billings and his exploits they would certainly never allow her to work anywhere near the Billingses' place.

Claire looked up at the overhead tree branches as she walked, and it was only then she remembered she'd ridden the bike that day. She'd left it leaning against the side wall at the B&B. She shook her head at her own forgetfulness. Maybe her older *schweschder* Sally would drive her to work tomorrow—if she could talk her into it.

Claire was the youngest of five children. The oldest child was a boy, Nathan, who was married, and her sister May, who was only two years older and in between Sally and herself, had married young. There were three of them left at home, herself and her *bruder* Elias and Sally, the eldest sister.

At times, Sally acted like she was the mother. Except she was bossy and cross whereas their mother was kind and sweet. Claire knew Sally was angry because she had no husband of her own and May already had *kinner*.

The farm had been in Claire's family for five generations, and one of her brothers would take it over when the time came for their father to retire. Convincing their father to retire any time soon wasn't going to be easy.

Although Claire had loved growing up on the farm, she envisioned a different life for her adult self. Her sister's husband owned a construction company, and May didn't have all the hard farm work to contend with that the farmers' wives had. All May did was keep house and raise her *kinner*. She had no worry about the weather and how it would affect the crops. All Claire hoped was that she didn't fall in love with a farmer.

Like all Amish girls, Claire had been taught how to run a household. Her hope was she would find the right man soon because she wanted children of her own while she was still young. She'd always been good with children, even when she was young, but she could never be a nanny like her friend Olive had been. She wanted to save looking after children until she had her own. For now, cleaning was the ideal way to pass the days until God found her a man. Besides helping her parents and getting herself a little pocket money, she got away from Sally and her increasingly bad moods.

Kicking a pebble ahead of her as she walked along the driveway, Claire wondered how to tell her parents she was working at the B&B. Maybe they wouldn't mind so much because Mrs. Wallen knew Mrs. Billings. There was only one thing for it; she would tell her *mudder* first, as soon as she got into the *haus,* and if it was all right with *Mamm,* it would be all right with her *vadder.*

Claire pushed the front door open and walked into the kitchen. Her *mudder* was in the middle of canning preserves with her older *schweschder* Sally.

"What are you doing home so early?" Sally asked, turning her chin up and looking down her nose, fixing her beady brown eyes on Claire.

When Claire had thought about telling her parents, she had forgotten all about her *schweschder*, who would most likely make a fuss of her news and not in a good way. Claire sat down at the kitchen table. "Mr. and Mrs. Wallen have their *dochder*-in-law insisting on doing their chores for them."

Her *mudder* raised her eyebrows and pinched her lips together.

"Gut," Sally said with a sharp nod of her head. "It was a silly idea for you five girls to do maids' work."

Claire and her four friends had all wanted to work, so they had taken out a stall some weeks ago at the farmers' markets to display their resumes—and they had all found employment.

"Does that mean you'll be helping us again?" Her *mudder* smiled, ignoring her oldest *dochder*'s remarks.

"Nee, Mamm, I've got another job. Mrs. Wallen recommended me to someone who owns a B&B. I went there today for an interview, and I start right away tomorrow."

Her *mudder* nodded. "That's *gut*. If Mrs. Wallen thinks they're okay, that's all right."

"You don't mind?" Claire asked.

She shook her head. *"Nee,* not if Mrs. Wallen knows them."

Sally stepped closer. "Does Mrs. Wallen know them or are you just making it up?"

"Jah, Sally, she does." She tried not to let any trace of irritation slip into her voice.

Sometimes their mother took a stall at the farmers' markets, and that was how *Mamm* had come to know Mr. and Mrs. Wallen; they always bought her mother's preserves and jams.

"What are the people like at your new job?" Sally asked.

"Jah, tell us about it."

Claire told her mother and sister as much as she knew about the B&B and everyone who worked there, leaving out the part about the owner's son.

"One job is as *gut* as another, I reckon," *Mamm* said.

"I think you should be home helping us," Sally said. Claire hung her head hoping her *mudder* would not agree.

"Hush now." *Mamm* frowned at Sally.

Claire was pleased with what her mother said, but dared not look her *schweschder* in the eye.

"Was that the place Jessie was working?" Sally asked.

"*Jah*, that's the one." Claire nodded.

Sally was not going to drop the subject. "Why did she leave?"

"I couldn't be sure. She doesn't want to work now she's got her mind on marrying Elijah." Claire rose to her feet. "I'm meeting the girls later at the coffee shop. Can I do anything before I go?"

Her *mudder* looked around the kitchen then said, "*Jah,* you can get the washing off the line."

Claire walked out of the kitchen and into the yard. "Be back in time to help with the dinner," Sally said.

"I was hoping you'd drive me to see the girls this afternoon."

Sally sighed. "All right, if I have to I will."

Chapter Two

All the way into town to meet the girls, Claire's older sister was grilling her over her new job. Claire did the best she could to answer her questions as calmly as she could. When Sally stopped the buggy outside of the Coffee House, Claire asked, "Can you collect me too?"

Sally rolled her eyes. "How am I supposed to fill in time? By the time I drive home, it'll be time to turn around and fetch you again."

Claire bit her lip hoping Sally wouldn't suggest she join them at the café. "It's okay. I'll have one of the girls give me a ride home."

"Good idea. If you get stuck, call me."

Claire jumped down from the buggy. *"Denke,* Sally."

Sally gave her a nod, and then moved the horse and buggy away.

Jessie was already there sitting down at their table. That was unusual—Jessie was nearly always the last one to arrive. Claire was just about to seize the opportunity of being alone with Jessie to tell her about her job, but then Olive and Amy walked in and Lucy came in a couple minutes later.

Dan hurried over once the five girlfriends were seated. "Good evening, ladies." He smiled. "What can I get you?" His question was to all of them, yet his eyes were fixed upon Lucy.

Once they all had given their orders, Dan walked away.

Claire made sure she was the first to speak. "I've got another job. I'm not working for Mrs. Wallen anymore. The Wallens have their *dochder*-in-law looking after them, but they recommended me to Mrs. Billings." Claire looked directly at Jessie. She had hoped she could tell her in private, but if she hadn't told her tonight, Jessie would've found out from someone else and that would have caused hurt feelings.

"At the B&B?" Jessie asked.

Claire nodded. "*Jah,* at the B&B. Cleaning, as you all know, wasn't my first choice, but it pays well and keeps me out of the *haus.*"

"Well, watch that Donovan Billings," Lucy said. "After all the things Jessie has told us."

"*Jah,* I'll be careful. I'll stay completely away from him," Claire said.

A waitress walked over with some of their food and drinks, followed by Dan holding another tray-full.

"Mrs. Billings is fair, but she expects a lot." Jessie picked up her knife and fork to eat the cake in front of her. She never ate with her fingers like the other girls.

"I'll manage—I hope." Claire giggled.

"You'll do well, Claire." Amy then asked the other girls, "Have any of you worked with Claire?"

"*Jah,* we've all worked together helping to clean old Mrs. Yoder's house when she was sick last summer," Jessie said. "Remember?"

"I thought I was the best at cleaning until I worked with Claire," Amy said.

Claire shrugged. "I just like to do things well."

Jessie put a hand softly on her friend's shoulder. "That's why you'll do a *gut* job for Mrs. Billings."

"*Denke,* Jessie. I'm glad you don't mind I'm working there right after you left."

Jessie replied, "I don't mind at all; just be sure you keep in mind what Lucy said."

The girls stayed and chattered for another two hours. When just Olive and Claire were left, Olive offered to drive Claire home without her having to ask.

As they walked to Olive's buggy, Claire asked, "Do you ever wonder what it's like away from the community, Olive?"

"I do, once in a while, but I don't think I'd like it. It seems cold and unfriendly. No one watches out for anyone and Blake said almost everyone is selfish. He didn't say it outright, but I gathered that from the stories he's told me."

Claire nodded, but there were times when she wondered what it would be like to live in one of the big cities. Sometimes it seemed a *gut* thing that no one would know who you were and they wouldn't be watching what you were doing.

Sometimes Claire wanted some privacy; being an *Englischer* would surely offer privacy. But then there would be no one to rely on in the bad times. As far as

Claire was concerned, that was the reason she was never going to leave, not for anything or anyone.

Olive looked over at Claire, and said jokingly, "You're not thinking of leaving, are you?"

"*Nee.* Sometimes I wonder what it would be like, but I'd never leave the community. Anyway, how are Blake and Leo?"

"Really good. He's started the instructions already."

"That's good. I'm so happy everything's worked out for you."

A smile beamed across Olive's face. "It was a miracle. I never saw myself with an Amish man. I never told anyone. In my heart, I must've known I'd marry a man who started off life as an *Englischer.*"

"*Jah,* maybe *Gott* put that knowledge into your heart. And soon, you'll be Leo's step*mudder.*"

"I know. I can hardly wait. He's not proposed yet, not properly. He said he will once he's been baptized."

They reached the buggy and climbed into it. Claire wondered who she'd marry. It was a subject that used to occupy most of her time. In more recent days she'd not been worrying too much about it, but now Olive was going to marry Blake, and Jessie would surely marry Olive's brother, Elijah. But who was left in the community for her? The only suitable man she could think of was Jessie's older brother, Mark, but, as nice as he was, she felt nothing for him.

When Claire walked into the B&B on her first day of work, Mrs. Billings was there to greet her. "Come through to my office, Miss Schoneberger."

Claire was tempted to correct the way Mrs. Billings

pronounced her name. After all, the first syllable was supposed to sound like "shone" as in "the sun shone" but Mrs. Billings labored the first part of her name with a dramatic "oh" sound. Claire thought better of correcting the older woman. She sat opposite Mrs. Billings as she had the previous day, with the white desk between them.

Mrs. Billings interlocked her perfectly manicured hands in front of her chin. "I don't really need another maid. When Jessie left, I employed someone else for four days a week. Do you know Jessie? She was one of your kind."

"Yes. Jessie's a good friend of mine." Claire chose to dismiss the "one of your kind" slight, crediting it to ignorance.

"I've decided to send you over to my son's house."

Claire held her breath. She'd been warned by Jessie about Donovan Billings and had set it in her mind to keep away from him, but here she was, on her very first day, being sent directly to his house.

Mrs. Billings continued, "He's just bought a house— Finch House. Do you know it?"

From the way Mrs. Billings spoke, Claire assumed Finch House must be a significant home or one of historic importance. "No, I haven't heard of it."

"It's well known around these parts, but I suppose you wouldn't have heard of it—being closed off in your community the way you are." Mrs. Billings peered down her nose at Claire. "Donovan is away for three more days, and I'd like you to clean his house for him and make it into a home. It'll be a nice surprise for him when he gets back."

Claire nodded and then tried to look grateful for the work. "Thank you, Mrs. Billings."

"Do you have transport?"

"I have my bike." Yes, she had her bike, if it was still where she'd left it yesterday when she'd forgotten it.

"Very well, it's not far from here. I'll pay you the same and not take into account the traveling time."

"Thank you, Mrs. Billings."

After Mrs. Billings had given Claire the key and directions to her son's house, Claire found her bike in the same place she'd left it. She wheeled it away from the house, stepped her leg over, then set off to find the address she'd been given.

After a fifteen-minute bike ride in the warm sunshine, Claire found Finch House. It was set well back from the road, but the sign on the gate saying "Finch House" confirmed she was at the right place. She wheeled her bike up the long gravel driveway.

Claire stared at Finch House unable to believe she was the lucky girl who got to clean it. It was beautiful, made of gray stone, with green shutters on the windows and surrounded by blooms of purple flowers.

She made her way closer, crossing a delightful curved bridge that stretched over a babbling stream. She stopped on the bridge and stared down to see tiny fish flitting around in the clear water. Stepping off the other end of the bridge she admired how meticulously the garden had been cared for, and she guessed Donovan would've had a gardener. Or he'd soon need one.

From what she could see of the outside, a large covered porch surrounded at least three sides of the house. A porch swing was positioned to the left of the front door, and white-painted wicker chairs and a matching table were on the other side. Claire leaned her bike against a tree while she wondered how the interior of the house would be.

She put the key in the lock and turned it, but it didn't work. Claire took a deep breath; she'd only just made it there and did not have the energy to ride all the way back just because Mrs. Billings had given her the wrong key. Claire took the key all the way out and rubbed it between her hands as if willing it to open the door. Kneeling down so the lock was at eye-level, she poked the key in as far as she could and, on a whim, turned it the opposite way. When it "clicked," she sighed with relief and stood up straight before she pushed the door open.

When she had stepped inside, she couldn't stop smiling. It was the sort of house she knew she'd never live in—it was far too grand. She could tell it was well over a hundred years old and maybe closer to two hundred. It never ceased to amaze Claire how *Englischers* were frivolous. What would a single man do with such a large house? It seemed a tremendous waste of space.

A musty smell of dust and damp invaded her nostrils. She screwed up her nose and her gaze fell to the floor. It was bluestone and slightly uneven as if it had been hand cut. She forged ahead, wanting to discover more of the interior.

The entrance led to a dining room on one side, where Claire was drawn to the view out through the glass double doors. She walked further and looked over the view of the gardens and saw that the water she'd crossed over had a waterfall at the other side.

She opened the doors to welcome in some clean air

and then proceeded to open all the doors and windows on the lower level.

The mustiness made it obvious no one had been in there for a long time. It was much better to use the fresh outdoor air than to use artificial scents. They just masked the odor, while the fresh air would sweep through taking the stale smell with it. She found the cleaning products in a room off from the kitchen.

Normally, she would have cleaned one room at a time, but she decided to sweep through with the vacuum first. She would attack the lower level first before she even looked at the others. The two living rooms had thick, old but beautiful carpets, which would be holding the smell, so cleaning them first would help make the place easier on the nose.

At Claire's home, they used a broom on their floorboards. They had smaller rugs that they took outside, and beat them on the line to force out the dust. She'd used an electric vacuum at Mrs. Wallen's place, so knew she could figure out this one. Pulling along the vacuum, Claire started from the front of the house to the back. It took her much less time than she thought, even though she was thorough.

As she walked through the place, she noticed there were knickknacks everywhere that were going to need a thorough dusting. Everything was nicely decorated, and she wondered whether Donovan had bought it like that. Again, she considered it didn't seem a place where a single man would live. She could not get a sense of who Donovan Billings was from his house.

Shaking her head, she focused on the job at hand. Even if he was the nastiest person in the world, she had agreed to work for Mrs. Billings for a year and she had to keep her word. She would be professional and not let what Jessie, or anyone else, said about Donovan bother her.

She'd always wanted her full-time job to be looking after her own husband and *kinner*. Now, it seemed more of a possibility since two of her friends were no longer single. She would meet someone who would complement her strengths and make up for her weaknesses— but, she reminded herself, it wouldn't happen until the time was right. Everything always happened in *Gott's* timing, and all she could do was be patient.

Since she had vacuumed through the whole lower level, she decided to first concentrate on the kitchen with the plan to move on into the living room. After she finished the living room, she decided she would break for lunch. With her cleaning projects planned, she walked to the kitchen pleased to notice the fresh air was doing its job of bringing the sweet scent of the garden flowers into the house.

She opened the fridge wondering whether she might have to clean it out, but it was clean, with hardly anything in it except an apple and a couple of bottles of wine.

Where was the kettle? When she found it, she plugged it in, checked that it worked properly, boiled it a couple of times to make sure there was no nastiness within and left it sitting open to dry. Fortunately, the kitchen did not need much cleaning. It appeared someone had already done that task, but it was someone less fastidious than she, as they had missed a couple of places. With those oversights remedied, she went into the living room and gazed over all the little knick-knacks. One of the things she hated more than anything was getting the cleaning cloth into the tiny crevices of such ornaments. Mrs. Wallen had many figurines too, which always gathered dust and grime.

At midday, Claire headed out to the porch for her break, taking the sandwiches she'd brought from home. Claire yawned and closed her eyes for just a moment.

"What the hell do you think you're doing?"

Claire jolted awake from a deep sleep, and opened her eyes. She jumped to her feet and put her hand on her chest as her heart beat uncontrollably. She'd fallen asleep on the porch. The angry young man in front of her had to be the Donovan Billings she'd heard so much about. She looked at his sullen face and searched for words.

Chapter Three

Claire cleared her throat. "I'm the maid."

"Maids are meant to clean, not sleep."

"I'm sorry. I've done a lot already."

"What have you been doing all day?" He shook his head, his lips twisting into a sneer as he stared at her. "I suppose my mother sent you over? She mentioned she'd send someone over, and I said no."

"I fell asleep. It's my lunch break, though." She hoped it was still her lunch break and she hadn't slept beyond that. "I've already cleaned a great deal of the house," she repeated as she struggled to hold back her tears. "I have done something. I didn't realize how tired I was when I sat down."

"How can you be tired when it's daytime? If you weren't so damned lazy, you would've been able to get a better job—because I can't imagine anyone wants to clean for a living. But your kind gets so little education none of you can get decent employment."

"Actually…" A tear trickled down her cheek, and

she quickly wiped it away. "If you'd go inside and have a look…"

"Look at what? Your imaginary work? Do you think I'm stupid?"

Claire hung her head. Her *mudder* had told her to remember when people showed anger they were hurt inside, and it rarely had anything to do with the person they were abusing. She looked up at him, now feeling sorry for him. "Do you want me to go away or shall I get back to work?"

He placed his hands on his hips. "I certainly don't want you, or anyone else, here when I'm not around. Do you understand?"

"Yes." She looked him in the eye, and he looked away from her.

"I suppose my mother gave you a key?"

"Yes."

Their eyes met again, and she could see exactly what the *Englischer* thought of her. She was less than he was because she was simply a maid, and an Amish maid at that.

He blew out a breath. "Fine, go on, finish what you came here to do." He walked into the house, and she followed.

She had a bit more to do on the lower level, and after that she would work her way up.

"What have you done to my clothes?" he snarled when he found her working in the living room over an hour later.

She shook her head. "I noticed a suitcase and I put the clothes away. Having a suitcase lying around was making things untidy, and the clothes inside would be wrinkled. My job, according to Mrs. Billings, is to clean and organize. I've hung all of your shirts and trousers in the wardrobe, your socks and other items are where they're meant to be, and I put your wallet in the drawer underneath that."

"After taking all the money from it?"

Claire sucked in her breath, horrified. "No, Mr. Billings, I would not do such a thing."

"Go back to my mother. I don't want you here." He walked into his bedroom and slammed the door.

When Donovan heard the front door shut, he came out of his room. He crept to the window, and looked out to see the young Amish woman riding her bike away from his house.

He covered his mouth. "What did I just do?" He knew he'd said horrible things to her; he'd hurt an innocent woman, who had seemed sweet-natured. "Taking my bad mood out on her wasn't fair and I should know better." Sighing, he ran a hand over his cropped hair. "When did I become this person?"

He turned and looked at how clean the house was. It smelled a whole lot better than it had before. He'd been far too busy to do anything to the house since he'd bought it.

The kitchen was spotless, apart from the mug in front of the kettle, which he knew she'd put there because he might want a hot drink. She was kind, and he had been a brute to her in return. He hadn't even asked her name. "If she comes back, I'm going to apologize. I can't treat people like that. Especially people who are nice to me, as they happen to be rare beings."

Donovan made himself a mug of coffee, feeling guilty the whole time. Although he'd insulted her, she hadn't retaliated. "How could I have chased her away like that?"

He sat on the porch, where she'd been, and tried not to think about her. He didn't like the person he'd become. The talks he'd had in New York about his franchising venture had gone well, and that was why he'd returned earlier than expected. His business life was thriving, but his personal life was a mess.

The coffee shop could run without him, but the restaurant always had upsets, and no one could sort out the problems but himself. He'd been certain he'd hired people who were capable of dealing with issues without having to call him constantly for assistance, but the calls came anyway. Donovan didn't dare take any time off. Now, though, he knew he didn't have any other choice. If he didn't take some time off, he was going to have a mental breakdown, and that would just make things a hundred times worse than they already were.

As he sipped his coffee, he thought about what his life might have been like if he hadn't opened the restaurant. He would've had a quiet life with just the coffee shop. Franchising was the obvious thing to do with the coffee shop, but the work in setting it up was exhausting. Why had he done this to himself?

The restaurant had to be run with a close eye on it. There was always a problem with over-ordering food; he had to keep a careful eye on that aspect of the business and as yet he could not let go of those reins completely.

Donovan knew he was going to have to visit his mother, which was something he was not looking forward to. Not when he knew the Amish maid would've reported how he'd acted toward her.

His phone vibrated in his pocket. *More than likely it'll be Mom or some problem at the restaurant,* he thought. He considered not answering it, but what if it was something important? The caller ID showed it was Declan. His head chef might've set the kitchen on fire, or something else just as urgent.

He pressed the "accept call" button. "Yes?"

"I thought you weren't going to answer." Declan sounded panicked. "We have a double booking."

Did he seriously have to do everything himself? "Okay, how did we come to have a double booking?" *Since when did a double booking become a major problem and an issue that the head chef was involved in rather than the booking manager?* "Who double booked it? Why did they double book it?" He sighed. "Give me as much information as you can and then we'll work out how to fix it."

"From the looks of things, it was Lily and Hannah." Lily had been fired last week for total incompetence. "Lily's was definitely the second booking, so I can tell Hannah she's going to get to keep her job."

"Hannah would never do something stupid."

"No, she wouldn't. Hannah booked in a party of ten, writing in that they wanted table twelve, and then Lily took the second one…although, the booking Lily's put in here is for an hour later, so she was technically working by the rules."

"The rules for small tables, yes, so this might've been a mistake." Donovan struggled not to yell at Declan and tell him to figure it out for himself. Why did they keep bothering him with all these nitpicking, trifling complications? The coffee shop was so much easier. Even though he was certain he'd taken all the staff through those rules more than once, they still couldn't work it out for themselves. "Do you think you can ring the second booking and ask them to come in half an hour later?"

"Maybe." Declan sounded hesitant.

"Why do you think you might not?"

"It looks like the second booking has a time constraint. They have to be here at that time because they have to be somewhere else in an hour, and if I were to ask them to come in later they might cancel."

"An hour? How much can they eat in an hour?"

"Um, I… I don't know."

"It's sounding ridiculous. There's something not right about that whole story. Who goes to a restaurant for a meal with a lot of people and books for just an hour? Just phone them and see what's up." Donovan shook his head; dinner was usually a minimum of two hours, not one hour. Who books a table for ten to "eat and run"? Donovan knew from his management training if his staff members were hopeless then he was mostly to blame. It was his lack of training them efficiently. Declan and Hannah were shaping up to be very competent, with a bit more experience and more thorough guidance from him. He remained calm and brushed a hand over his hair. He would have to train them better, but where would he find the time or the patience? "They're both tens?"

"Yeah…yes, definitely both tens. Oh, I think I know what you're thinking."

"We have a back room for a reason. Did the second booking stipulate a table?"

"Doesn't look like it. Could be Lily didn't write it down, so I'll ring them and make certain it's okay for us to put them in the back room."

"Only call me back if there's a huge problem."

"Okay, Boss, and thanks."

When Declan hung up, Donovan glared at his phone. He had a horrible feeling it was going to ring again. He wanted to spend some time drinking his coffee and thinking about how he was going to fix things with the pretty Amish maid, which might not be possible.

The last thing he wanted was to make people hate him. Unfortunately, he often did that when he took his anger out on people who didn't deserve it. Things hadn't gone well with Jessie and that was something he regretted.

Sighing, Donovan sipped his coffee. He was going to change; he had to change. If he didn't, he was going to lose good people, people who were suffering because he hadn't taken the time to train them.

The phone rang again, and he snarled at it. He knew from the caller I.D. it was the restaurant again. "Yes?"

"We've had a problem with the supplier." It was Declan again. "And they say they're not going to deal with anyone who isn't you, even though I've told them you aren't in today, and I'm the head chef."

"What's the problem?"

"They've sent us the wrong lobster order."

"Did they send us frozen again?"

"Yes."

"When I come back, we're going to change the supplier. They're useless." Donovan sighed. "I've got their number in my phone; I'll call them and sort it out, then I'll let you know what's happening."

"Sorry about this."

"Not your fault, Declan. You're not responsible for their inefficiency."

"True. Thanks for understanding that. Talk to you soon."

Donovan's pet peeve was ordering seafood at a restaurant only to find they used frozen rather than fresh. He hated serving the customers at his restaurant frozen seafood. He would feed them fresh or not have any on the menu at all.

Donovan pressed the number for the supplier. "Good afternoon, this is Donovan Billings and I've just been in contact with my restaurant and they tell me you've sent us frozen lobsters—yet again—when we always order them fresh. In fact, we have a standing order for fresh and yet this is not the first time you've sent us the imported lobsters, which are frozen. I'm beginning to get ticked off with your constant mistakes. We order the same thing every other day. How can you get it wrong nine times out of ten?"

A young woman on the other end of the phone did her best to console him. "Mr. Billings, I'm sorry we sent the wrong ones. We've got new staff on."

"I've spoken to you before, haven't I?"

"A couple of times, yes." She sighed. "I've just ordered the lobsters to be replaced and you'll get them rush-delivered this afternoon. Once again, I apologize. You're one of our best customers and I'll personally make sure it doesn't happen again."

"I'll let my chef know the order is on its way. Can I authorize Declan Jones to speak on my behalf next time? He's my head chef, and I'm not always available."

"Of course, I'll put him on the list."

Once Donovan ended the call, he sent a text message to Declan, pleased he had been able to put out another fire, and without leaving home.

Chapter Four

"Can I see you for a moment, Mrs. Billings?"

"Back already, Claire?"

"Your son arrived and wasn't too pleased to see me and told me I should come back." Claire hoped Mrs. Billings had work for her elsewhere, or she'd be out of a job on her very first day.

"I didn't expect him back so soon." Mrs. Billing raised her eyebrows. "I'll have a talk with him. He seems to have this notion in his head he can do everything himself. I keep telling him he needs to delegate, or he'll send himself to the lunatic asylum." Mrs. Billings looked Claire up and down. "I'll take you to Linda; she'll find you something to do for the rest of the day." Mrs. Billings patted Claire on her arm. "I'll talk to my son and fix it for you to go back there tomorrow. He won't be home; he leaves early."

"Will it be all right with him if I go back there?" Claire didn't want to get yelled at again.

"I'll call him and make sure of it. Someone needs to clean the place and he knows it won't be me—and I know it won't be him." She chuckled. "Come with me and I'll find Linda."

Claire knew from Jessie's stories Linda was one of the housekeepers and a nice lady.

"Can I tell you something, Mrs. Billings?"

"Yes, of course; what is it?"

"Your son was angry because I fell asleep on his porch, but I was on my lunch break." She thought it better to get in first to tell her of her mistake. It would sound worse if she were to hear it from someone else.

Mrs. Billings regarded her carefully. "I appreciate your honesty; that is a rare commodity these days." Mrs. Billings turned around and kept walking down the hallway. "Don't take my son's anger as a personal attack. He's that way with everyone. I can't say I blame him for being upset with you. You certainly can't fall asleep again, even if it is during your lunch break."

"No, of course not, Mrs. Billings. It won't happen again."

The very next day, Claire knocked on the door of Finch House. Mrs. Billings had directed her to go straight there in the morning. Claire hoped Mrs. Billings had talked to her son, and that there wasn't going to be a repeat of yesterday's behavior.

When no one answered a second round of knocking, she put the key in the lock, remembering to turn it the opposite way other keys turn, and when she heard the click she opened the door and entered the house. Even though she'd been told Donovan wasn't going to be home, it felt like a weight had been lifted from her shoulders when she saw he wasn't there.

She went straight to the kitchen, which was a mess already. There was sugar all over the counter and bits of food everywhere. Claire was unable to believe someone was quite so messy. Once she'd cleared the mess, she checked the living room. Seeing it was tidy, she walked up the steps to the second-level bathroom. With Donovan not there, she was determined to get a whole lot done, so he wouldn't have a further bad opinion of her.

After the bathroom was clean, she moved on to the bedrooms. Her mistake of falling asleep on the job was going to be her last mistake. Once the bedrooms were done, she cleaned all the windows. Had she been working for anyone else, she would've made herself a cup of tea. As it was Donovan's house, the last thing she wanted was for him to come in and find her having a cup of tea. He would surely think she was slothful.

Now in an upstairs study, she dusted some framed photos that hadn't been there the day before. She picked up a photo of Donovan. He looked like he'd been a happy person at one point. If only she could wind back the clock. It wasn't good she'd got on the wrong side of the boss's son.

Biting on her lip, she placed the photo back where it had been and turned her attention to vacuuming the place again even though she'd done it the day before. She realized cleaning this house could be a full-time job because once she got to the end she'd have to start all over.

Being back at the same house today made her think of the disgust in Donovan's eyes when he had found her asleep. Then he had talked down to her for being a maid, and he apparently had a problem with the Amish.

Pushing the vacuum around was another job out of the way. Her parents had brought her up to be hard-working; they always said to "do everything heartily as unto *Gott*."

Giving another sigh, she noticed a smear on one of the windows and gave it a quick wipe. Then she found herself staring out the window at the wonderful gardens and the birds flitting from branch to branch in the trees. It was the sort of view she'd love to have from her room at home. From her bedroom at home, she could see almost the entire farm and to the end of the street; she could see who was visiting before they even arrived.

Then her thoughts turned to Donovan again and she knew she shouldn't have let his rudeness get to her. Maybe she had to toughen up and get used to the *Englischers* if she was to work for them. At least Mrs. Billings had been nice enough to her about falling asleep on Donovan's porch. From what Jessie had said about her, Claire would have thought she might be sterner about such a lapse.

She hated admitting she was finding herself attracted to Donovan's unusual good looks, considering the way he was. From Jessie's warnings, she had thought he'd be charming and polite.

Chapter Five

Claire was washing her hands in the downstairs bathroom when she heard a car. She walked to the kitchen window to see Donovan closing his car door. She swallowed a lump in her throat as her heart accelerated, hoping his mother had spoken to him about his behavior.

Does he even know I'm here today? I hope his mother told him I'd be here.

It was best, she considered, to meet him at the front door. When she opened the door, he smiled at her. "Oh, I was hoping you'd be here. Look, I'm sorry about my rudeness yesterday. It was unforgivable."

With relief, Claire said, "That's quite all right, I forgive you. I hope your mother told you I'd be back here today."

"Yes. Yes, she did. You did a wonderful job yesterday." Claire smiled, glad he was in a better mood today.

He stepped through the door and walked into the center of the house. "So, what do you think of the old place?" His eyes traveled around the living room.

"It's such a beautiful house and I love the garden."

"Yes, the garden is quite magical. It's the kind of place fairies and goblins would live." He coughed.

Claire smiled at him. It was something a child might say. Was this his way of being charming, or was he trying to make up for yesterday?

"The inside needs modernizing."

Claire looked around and wondered what he thought needed modernizing. "I think it's lovely the way it is."

He shook his head. "No, it's too dated. Of course, it's a very old house, but even the grandest old houses have modern kitchens and bathrooms. I'm having a new kitchen put in next week. It's costing me eighty grand." Donovan looked pleased with himself.

Claire gasped. "Did you say eight or eighty?"

"Eighty."

"How could a kitchen cost so much?"

"Everything's imported—the marble, the appliances—everything. The stove alone cost just under twenty-five and that was wholesale. When I'm done, I'll have the most amazing dinner parties here."

It was a waste as far as Claire was concerned. She had been brought up to be frugal. In her opinion, the current kitchen was perfect, and she saw no reason to throw money away on a new one.

He dipped his head down. "You don't look impressed."

"Am I supposed to be?"

He laughed. "I guess so. It'll be nice when it's finished."

"But, Mr. Billings, it's nice now."

"What's your name?"

"I'm Claire Schoneberger."

"Well hello, Claire Schoneberger."

Claire smiled, pleased they were finally speaking like two human beings. "Hello, Mr. Billings."

He swiped a hand through the air. "No 'Mr.' Just Donovan, please."

"Donovan then."

"Would you make me a cup of hot tea?"

"Yes." She turned away from him to fill the kettle. "I hope you don't think I'm rude, but I don't see the sense of spending so much money when this kitchen is lovely. Well, it's more than perfectly all right, I think it's beautiful."

"Beauty, Claire, is in the eye of the beholder."

She plugged the kettle into the wall and turned to him. "I'm sorry; it's not my place to comment."

"You Amish are a different breed, that's for sure."

Claire ignored his comment and opened the cupboard to see what kind of tea he had.

"The green tea is in the cupboard on the far left. Would you join me in a cup?"

"Okay." Claire was anxious to get on with the cleaning, but figured since he was being nice she could be too.

"As long as you don't fall asleep, because that's what you seem to do on your breaks."

Claire looked at him to see he was smiling. "I'm sorry. It'll never happen again." She smiled back, pleased he was making an effort to put her at ease.

"Don't be so sorry. I was rude, and you remained polite. You made me see what an idiot I am."

"I'm sure you're not an idiot."

"Do you know Jessie Miller?"

Claire looked at the kettle that had just boiled. "Yes, she's a very good friend."

"How's she doing?"

"She's very well." Claire poured hot water over the teabags waiting in their two cups. "I don't use teabags very often. I normally use loose tea from a teapot." Claire knew Jessie had liked Donovan, and it seemed he'd been fond of her too, but now Jessie was with Elijah.

"Probably tastes better that way."

"I think so."

Donovan took the two cups in his hands. "Shall we sit at the table?"

"Yes. Can I get you something to eat, Donovan?"

"There's nothing much here. I eat out mostly."

"That's right, you own a restaurant and a café. I suppose you'd have the choice of eating at either place."

He spun around, nearly spilling the hot drinks. "Jessie told you about me?"

"Not really. She just mentioned you have a coffee shop café and a restaurant."

"What else did she say?"

Claire shrugged her shoulders. "That's about it." She then followed Donovan to the long table in the formal dining room. He pulled out a chair for her and one for himself. "This is a very grand room," Claire said, as she sat down. She watched him sit next to her and then he took a sip of tea.

He looked into her eyes. "I fell in love with her as soon as I saw her."

She was transfixed by him and couldn't look away.

No wonder Jessie had fallen for him. "You fell in love with…" Her voice trailed off quizzically.

"With the house, I mean, when I saw her. I had to have her. She just needs modernizing. This'll be a real home where I can stay forever. Let me give you a tour." He pushed out his chair and stood up. "Let's go."

"What about our tea?"

"It's too hot. Come on, I'll show you some things you haven't seen."

Claire giggled a little at his energy. She'd already seen the house, so she didn't know what he planned to show her.

They walked out through the back door, past the fishpond and waterfall. "There's a magical view up further."

As they walked, he pointed out particular flowers and trees. Claire was impressed he knew their Latin botanical names.

"The original house was built in seventeen hundred, and additions were built in around the eighteen forties. There are five bedrooms and three and a half bathrooms, but you already know that. It appears a newer outer structure has been built around the older original house. I'm pretty sure the three fireplaces were rebuilt along with more bedrooms at that time. Not so long ago there was a vineyard here. There are twenty-eight acres of land."

"What are you going to do with all the land?"

He raised his eyebrows. "The neighbor on the southern side has used most of the land for grazing and part of it for corn crops. I'm thinking of keeping things the same. When I bought the house, the lease on the land was ongoing and it has two years before it runs out. I figured I'd leave things be and renew the lease if the neighbor wants to continue." They reached the top of the hill. He put his hands on his hips. "Well, what do you think of this?"

She stepped up next to him and looked around. "You can see for miles. It's beautiful."

"It certainly is." He pointed to the house. "It's a good view of the house from here."

"You can see how large it is. Much bigger than I thought it was. Are those barns yours?" Claire pointed to three barns to the left of them.

"Yes, they're mine, but they're part of the lease to Mr. Watkins next door."

"You must feel a sense of accomplishment you've got all this at such a young age." Again, she could see why Jessie had a secret crush on him. He was dynamic and, when he wanted to be, charming.

He scoffed. "No, it's never enough."

Claire raised her eyebrows at the concern on his face. What was it that pushed him to want more when he had so much already?

When he looked at her, the worry left his face. "What do you think of all the flowers?"

"They're beautiful. I love flowers."

"All women love them." A little noise sounded from the back of his throat. "Something told me you would. I'm going to have to get a gardener, aren't I?"

Claire laughed and nodded. "And pretty quickly if you don't already have one."

Donovan gazed around his land once more. "This place gives me a sense of peace. I was brought up in a large city, and then Mom and I moved here when Dad died. I was twelve at the time."

"I'm sorry to hear that. What was your father like?"

"He worked hard. He had hotels, which meant late nights. He died suddenly of a heart attack. It was a shock. Here one minute and gone the next. I mean, he had no signs of illness."

"I'm sorry."

He looked at her. "I'm an only child. I think it's easier for people who have siblings."

Claire thought of her own siblings. Out of her two siblings still at home, Elias was certainly a blessing, but Sally was hard work. But still, she knew Sally would support her in a crisis. "Yes, I think you're right."

"You've got brothers and sisters?"

"I've got two brothers and two sisters. One brother and one sister are married and the other two still live at home."

"I suppose you get on with them all just fine?"

Claire laughed. "Funny you should ask. My oldest sister, Sally, is always checking up on me and always finds fault. She tries to run my life."

He smiled. "Maybe the reality of having siblings isn't as good as imagining it."

"No, it's good."

"I'd like to have a lot of children."

Again, another thing Jessie would've liked if he'd shared that information with her. "You would?"

He moved his weight from one foot to the other. "Why do you look surprised?"

"I didn't see you as someone who'd want a family.

You seem to be… I thought you'd be too focused on your businesses."

"Did Jessie tell you that?"

She laughed. "No, not at all." He sniggered.

"I think our tea would be cool enough to drink now," she said, feeling a sudden pang of nerves.

"Okay, after you." As they walked back to the house, he asked, "And how many children would you like?"

"As many as *Gott* gives me."

"No, really. Don't you have an ideal number?"

She swung to face him. "Four. Two girls and two boys is my ideal number."

"Really? Me too." They both laughed.

"I'd reckon in your community four is a small number of children."

"Yes, there are a lot of families with eight and ten and even more."

"That would make for pretty cramped living, I'd dare say."

"Not only that, a lot of our families have grandparents live with them. I've heard that doesn't happen outside the community too much."

"Some people take their grandparents in, but you're right, it's not common."

When Claire had left, Donovan turned off his phone and sat on the porch with a gin and tonic. It irked him Jessie was now dating Elijah. What had Jessie really said to Claire about him?

He knew Elijah and Jessie liked each other the moment he'd seen them together outside the B&B. He'd lost Jessie, he knew it, but was he getting a second chance with Claire? Although he didn't believe in God, he'd always wanted a woman who had good morals and ethics to bring up his children and be his partner in life. An Amish girl would be perfect for him and maybe this was his second chance, with Claire.

Donovan was through with women who wanted the richest man they could find and expected to be showered with gifts. He laughed out loud when he thought maybe he wanted a good woman to balance out the bad in himself. With the next woman he got close with, he'd be a different man. Next time, he'd be the best person he could be. None of the women he'd met at nightclubs were the kind of women he'd settle down with. He took a gulp of his drink and felt guilty for switching off his phone. From there, his mind ran away with him as he imagined what emergency would be taking place at the restaurant. Had they double-booked again, had one of the trainee chefs accidently caused a fire? Whatever it was, they'd have to handle it themselves.

He thought back to the look on Claire's pretty face when he'd mentioned renovating the kitchen. She'd caught him out. Yes, she was supposed to be impressed with the amount he was spending on renovations. That showed him he was going about things the wrong way.

A year ago, he'd dated a different girl every week. Mostly a "relationship" with a girl would last three weeks; that was the average time and then it ended. Those kinds of relationships did not appeal to him any longer. Maybe he was getting old or gaining some sense.

As he watched two birds playing and chirping in the tree in front of him, he realized he didn't know when he was going to see Claire again. He recalled how awful he'd been the previous day. It was a wonder she hadn't quit then and there. No one deserved to be treated like that. No wonder the poor girl had fallen asleep. She'd worked so hard on the place; then he came along and reprimanded her instead of thanking her. Then he replayed all the things he'd said to Jessie, hoping Jessie hadn't told Claire.

There was something more about Claire. She had an inner strength, and he'd seen that the very first time he'd laid eyes on her. Since he certainly couldn't ask her out for a meal, he had to find a clever way to see more of her—but how?

He turned his phone on and called his mother. She answered immediately. "Mom, have you got the maid coming back to my place again tomorrow?"

"No, I told her to come here. Do you want her again tomorrow?"

"Yes, I've got a few things that have to be done. Lots of unpacking to do, and such. On second thought, could you have her go to the restaurant first?"

"All right."

"The cleaners aren't coming in tomorrow and I'll need her."

"Okay. She's gone now. I'll send her there tomorrow as soon as she comes in."

He reminded himself to be more thoughtful of others. He'd have to change if he wanted a special woman who was good and kind. "Oh, and, Mom?"

"Yes?"

"Thank you for sending me a maid. It was very thoughtful."

There was silence before she answered. "You're wel-

come. And I only did it as a surprise. I hadn't expected
you back for a few more days."

Donovan hung up pleased with himself for remembering to thank his mother. He knew mostly he'd taken
her for granted. He then called his restaurant cleaners
to cancel their early-morning clean. Then he texted the
manager and told him to arrange the staff to clean not
only the kitchen, but also the whole restaurant, before
they went home tonight.

He chuckled over his plan as he turned and pressed
the button of his phone to off.

Rarely did he thank his mother for anything. She'd
been a good mother, and things had been hard for her
when his father died, leaving her with a twelve-year-
old son. He'd been strong-willed from childhood, and
his mother was the same, which was why they clashed.

The sun had disappeared behind the trees when Donovan thought about dinner. There was no food in the
house, but he'd rather go hungry than go to the restaurant and hear about all the problems. In his car, he dug
a couple of protein bars from his gym bag and quickly
munched on those, and followed them with an energy
drink normally saved for after a training session.

When night came, the quiet was deafening. He was
rarely home during the evening and didn't even own a
television or a radio.

His mind strayed again to Claire. She was exactly
the kind of woman he wanted to marry and he was determined to know more about her. If she was as she appeared, he'd make the effort to win her heart.

Chapter Six

The next morning, Claire went back to work not knowing whether she'd be sent back to Donovan's house. There was more work to be done at his house, but Mrs. Billings had told her to report to the B&B.

She found Mrs. Billings sitting next to Yvonne, the receptionist. "I'm loaning you out to my son today at his restaurant. His cleaners let him down this morning," Mrs. Billings said.

Claire nodded. "Okay, shall I go there now?"

"Yes, he's waiting. Hurry along."

Once she walked through the back door of the restaurant, Donovan was nowhere to be seen. "Donovan?" she called out.

"In here."

She followed his voice and found him in the kitchen. "Thank you for coming over, Claire." Donovan ran a hand over his hair. "There's always something going wrong in this place. Every day there's another drama, another problem. I don't know why it can't be like the coffee shop, which practically runs itself."

Claire had no idea what to say. The stress was evident from his face and she didn't want to upset him by saying something inappropriate. "Where do you want me to start?"

He blew out a huff of air. "And again, I don't know why I'm here so early. I've got a manager; he's the one who should be here. He's useless, completely useless."

Claire sucked her lips in and kept quiet.

Donovan looked at her. "I'm sorry; I always seem to be complaining about something."

Claire smiled.

"The staff clean the kitchen before they go. They have to; it's health regulations, and besides, they'd lose their jobs if I found one speck of dust, leftover food or dirt in the kitchen." He opened the ovens and looked in the fridges; then he walked toward the dining area. "It's the floors, the chairs and the tables. I need all the chairs wiped down. Then they go up on the tables for the floor to be washed."

"Okay, I can do that. Where do I find the cleaning equipment?"

"Over here." He opened a door to a room adjacent to the kitchen.

Claire said, "I'll get started."

"Thanks, Claire, you're a lifesaver."

Claire giggled. Soon, Donovan was gone.

The dining room was a large area and seated one hundred and twenty people. When she finished, she went to find Donovan not knowing whether she should lock the building before she left. Before she could find him, the kitchen staff came through the door.

Minutes later, six staff were milling around the

kitchen. None of them spoke to her. Since she had finished the cleaning and packed the equipment away, she walked out the door and headed back to the B&B. On the walk, she wondered if Mrs. Billings had enough work to keep her employed since she was being sent here and there. Then she remembered her pledge to Mrs. Billings; she'd stay for twelve months. But, would she keep her employed for twelve months if there wasn't enough work?

"Finished, Claire?"

Claire turned to see Donovan getting out of his car.

"Yes, I have. Your chefs and the rest of the staff seem to be there. I'm going to see what Mrs. Billings wants me to do if that's okay."

He shook his head. "No, I've borrowed you again for the day. I'm your boss today."

She walked to him. "What shall I do?"

"Come with me."

He opened his car door on the passenger side. When she hesitated, he said, "Come on; I won't bite."

Claire let out the breath she was holding and slipped into the low leather seat. "Are we going back to your place again?"

"I'm afraid so. Being a bachelor, I've got a lot of work piled up. I've got loads of washing and I need things organized."

"Yes, I can do that."

When the car pulled up at Finch House, Claire was secretly pleased she was back there. She hoped she could spend time in the gardens before she left. "Are you staying here or going out again?"

"I'm working from home. I've a ton of paperwork

and doing it here is as good a place as any." He got out of the car.

Claire followed him as he strode toward the house. She looked up at the sky to see it was gray. "I don't know if it's a good idea to do the washing today; it looks as though it's going to rain."

He unlocked the door then turned to face her. "That's why us modern people have electricity, so we can have things like clothes dryers."

"You have one of those?"

"Yes, didn't you see it in the laundry room?"

"Maybe. I didn't take much notice."

He chuckled. "You throw the washed clothes in and push a button." He held the door open for her to walk through. "I'm sorry if I sounded harsh; I didn't mean to come across as though I was belittling you or your people."

Claire laughed. "I've had worse said to me. I didn't think you were being mean. It's okay."

His face relaxed. "I've put all the washing in the laundry room. As soon as you put the washing machine on, you can go through the house and organize my closets and dressers, starting at my bedroom."

Claire's eyes flickered to the floor at the mention of his bedroom.

He stepped toward her. "Don't concern yourself; I'll be out here working at the dining table."

She nodded and walked into the laundry. She figured out how to work the washing machine and, after she'd divided the laundry by color and filled it with the first load, she pressed the "start" button and headed to his bedroom.

His closets were now a mess and there were more boxes and suitcases. She decided where things should go and went to work. An hour and a half later, she had his room organized, the first washing machine load in the dryer and the next load of washing on. Then she moved on into one of the many extra bedrooms. This room was cluttered with overcoats and heavier clothes including bulky sweaters.

When she had done all the bedrooms and the two bathrooms, she went to speak to Donovan. "All done. I've cleaned and organized the bedrooms and all the bathrooms, and the laundry room. I haven't touched the upper level yet. Do you want me to show you where I've put everything?"

Without looking up, he said, "I'll figure it out. Why don't you make us some lunch?"

"With what? Have you been shopping?"

He looked up. "No, I haven't and that's what I need to do. I had to starve last night, which goes against my religion." He chewed on the end of a pencil. "I don't want to go to the restaurant every night and have to figure out their issues." Donovan threw the pencil down. "Let's make a quick trip to pick up some food."

"You want me to go with you?"

He jumped to his feet. "Yes. Let's go."

When Donovan had said a "quick trip," Claire had no idea he meant he would speed in the car.

"You're going quite fast." Claire hung on to the armrest.

He looked over at her. "I'm sorry. I'll go slower. I'm

used to doing everything fast these days. I get over-whelmed sometimes, I've got so much to do."

"Can't someone else help you?"

"Yes, but then there are some things only I can do." He glanced at her again. "If you could drive I could've sent you out to get food."

"I could have ridden my bike."

He smirked. "Do you think that would be a good solution?"

She giggled. "No."

"Do you ride everywhere?"

"Most days."

He gave a sideways glance. "No wonder you're so slim."

Claire ignored his comment. "Is it necessary to be so stressed when you work hard? I mean, can't you do what you do without it upsetting you?"

"That's the only way I know to get things done. I work myself into a frenzy that I've got to get something done and then I do it. Right now, I'm working on get-ting one of my businesses franchised, and then when the money starts coming in I'll be able to relax."

"That's good."

"Yes, I'm on track to be a millionaire by the time I'm thirty. I've had no help. Well, maybe a little bit from Mom." He looked over at her. "Not impressed?"

"No. I'm happy for you if that's what you want."

He stopped the car in the parking lot at the grocery store and turned his body to face her. "And what do you want, Claire?"

Claire smiled as she thought of what she wanted.

"To have my own home, my own little family and to be happy."

"Is that all?"

"That's everything. It is to me anyway."

He studied her carefully. "Let's go. Help me choose some food." They walked into the supermarket and he picked up a basket just inside the door.

"You're not going to get much?"

Donovan shook his head. "Just enough for a couple of days. Then I'll come back and get some more."

"It would save time if you bought more now. I mean, you're here. It would save some trips."

He breathed out heavily. "Very well." Donovan changed his basket for a grocery cart.

"Don't look so worried; we'll be quick." Claire took hold of the cart and whizzed around the store filling it up. Donovan followed behind and grunted his approval or disapproval every time Claire asked his opinion on something. "That's it then. That didn't take long."

Donovan looked at the full cart. "Thank you, Claire. This was a good idea. It'll be good to have basic food in the cupboard."

"You're welcome." It was good to have his approval.

After the groceries had been processed through the checkout, Donovan wheeled the cart to the car.

"We've got already-cooked beef and I can make potato salad for lunch."

"Sounds like that'll take a long time. Let's just get

something in there." Donovan nodded to a small diner next to the food mart.

Claire only agreed because she was hungry, and besides, refusing might be impolite.

Chapter Seven

They ordered two hamburgers with the works. Donovan put his elbows up on the table and clasped his fingers together while he stared at Claire.

Seeing him smile, she asked, "Have I done something funny?"

He shook his head. "No, but this isn't getting my work done. And you know what? I don't even care."

"Once you've got food in your stomach you'll be able to work better. Can I help you with anything when we get back?"

"You're helping me enough by getting my life organized."

"I wouldn't say I'm doing that. I've just rearranged some closets."

The waitress brought their sodas and hamburgers to the table.

Donovan lifted the top of his bun and looked at what was inside. "It must be comforting to live in a community such as yours."

Claire nodded. "It is, but some people feel it's too restrictive, like their life is mapped out."

"Is that how you feel?" He took a mouthful of hamburger.

"I just sometimes wonder, what if my life doesn't turn out the way it's supposed to?"

He frowned and when he swallowed, he asked, "What do you mean? Do you mean there aren't any men your age in the community?"

Claire giggled and put her fingers to her mouth. "How would you know that?"

Donovan laughed. "Your friend, Jessie, happened to mention it. She only said it in passing, but I believe she's found someone now?"

"Yes, Elijah. Elijah who's doing the work for you at the B&B."

"Yes, I know."

"He is the brother of one of our good friends."

"And what will you do, Claire? You want to have a family, so how do you plan to do that seeing there are no men in the community for you to choose from?"

Claire scrunched her shoulders up. "I'm leaving it up to God."

"Ah, so you're ignoring the issue."

She frowned at him. "No. I'm simply not allowing my faith to waver."

"For how long are you going to leave it up to God?"

The bishop was right when he said not to associate with those out of the community. She really had nothing in common with Donovan. Besides that, he was putting doubts in her mind. She'd fought hard to rid her mind of such doubts. "As long as it takes."

"You do know after the age of thirty it's difficult for women to have children?"

Her mouth fell open. "I'm nowhere near thirty." Is that what he thought?

"What if you get older and there are still no men in the community for you?"

Claire took a bite of her hamburger, so she would have time to think of an answer. When she finished it, she said, "It will be God's will so it won't matter."

He nodded. "Everything is God's will whether good or bad?"

She frowned. "Are you trying to trick me?"

Donovan shook his head. "No, I'm simply trying to understand some things."

"The answer is 'yes.' We can pray about things, but God knows the beginning and the end. Something we pray for might not be good for us, and God knows that—He can see how the end will be."

"Well, I know what's good for me." He took a last bite of his burger.

Claire hurried to finish her food, so he wouldn't complain about how long she took to eat, because, *Time is money.*

The waitress came hurrying back to their table. "Have you folks heard about the severe storm watch and the tornado watch?"

"No," Donovan said.

"The weather service has issued a watch for severe storms and possibly a tornado. They say this area is almost certain to be hit. We're closing up pretty soon." The waitress left them to speak to other patrons.

Donovan jumped to his feet, left money on the table and grabbed Claire by the arm. "Let's go."

Once they were driving away, Claire said, "We haven't had one of those in a while. They usually issue so many of these watches, and then nothing happens. A little wind and rain at most."

"Doesn't matter. I'm driving you home."

"Okay, *denke*."

"I'd feel safer if you were with your family."

Claire would feel safer too because all her family and the community prayed for safety. Claire looked out the car window to see the sky had changed from blue to an eerie shade of greenish-gray. "Where are you going?"

"Me? I guess I'll go back home. It'll probably amount to nothing. You're right. Most of these tornados fizzle out before anything happens and it just ends up being a thunderstorm or a heavy rain."

"It's down this road here and to the left. You can leave me here if you wish; I can walk the rest of the way."

"I've come this far I might as well drive you all the way." Claire was thinking more of herself than his convenience.

She didn't want Sally to see her driven home by a handsome *Englischer*.

He ducked his head to look at her house when he stopped outside it. "Keep safe."

She opened the car door and turned around to say goodbye. "Will you be all right?" Claire was sure there was a flicker of a moment between them as they looked into each other's eyes.

"Of course. I'll see you tomorrow. Now I know

where you live; I'll fetch you at nine because you rode your bike today, didn't you?"

"I did. Where are you going to shelter?"

"I'll go back to the house." He reversed the car without giving Claire any time to protest. Was there a storm shelter there? She hadn't seen one.

Light rain forced her into the house. Her family had already heard about the weather alert, now raised to a tornado warning. They'd secured everything, and their domestic animals were enclosed in the barn. Claire was grateful Sally said nothing about who had brought her home.

As he drove away from Claire's house, Donovan saw the clouds were darkening further and the daylight was turning a very odd green. The safest place might be in his house rather than the restaurant. He called his mother to make sure she knew about the tornado. Then he called his staff at the restaurant and the café and told them to close up and get everyone to shelter.

There might've been a lot of tornado watches and warnings, but something told Donovan this one was going to be more than just a watch or a fizzled warning, even though he'd acted in front of Claire as though he wasn't worried. Despite his mother's pleadings to go to her place, he insisted on going back to Finch House.

He parked his car in the newly built four-car garage, which was slightly away from the house. He considered staying in the garage but opted to find a safe place within the house. There was no basement, so he knew the safest place during a tornado was the center of an interior room or in a hallway, avoiding windows and doors. If things got really bad, he could get under the dining table, which was a solid piece of wood. He could even push the table into the hallway so it was away from windows and doors.

His phone beeped. He looked at the caller I.D. and saw it was his mother again. "Yes, Mom?"

"I've been listening to the storm reports; it's not looking good. Come here and shelter in the basement with me."

"No, Mom, I'm okay here. Just make sure you're safe, okay?" The phone clicked in his ear. She tended to end conversations abruptly when she didn't get her way.

He had no radio in his house, so he tried to download an app on his phone to hear news of the approaching storm.

Finding he'd just lost service, he groaned and placed his phone in his pocket.

Remembering the food still in the trunk, he pulled on a heavy jacket and hurried to the car to get the bulk of the shopping bags out. If some emergency happened, at least he'd have food. The gym workouts were paying off. With six bags of groceries in his hands, he made his way back to the house under a sky as black as night.

As soon as he closed his front door and dumped the food in the kitchen, he tried the lights. At that instant a streak of lightning flashed across the sky and its immediate thunderclap made him jump. The electricity had gone out. Donovan got a flashlight from the kitchen drawer and knew it was time to take shelter.

He grabbed his useless phone and sat on the floor in the hallway with his flashlight, and waited for the power to come back on. It was a short time later when he was dozing off he heard things banging against the outside of the house. The wind was howling and large objects were hitting the house. He hoped his old house would hold up against the storm. It had been weathering storms for hundreds of years; was this storm going to be the one to take it down?

Suddenly, all went quiet. It was an eerie, dead silence and Donovan knew he was in the eye of the storm. There was an almighty crash and Donovan was surrounded by debris. He looked up in horror to see the front part of his house was gone. He bolted down the hall toward the bathroom as he was deluged with water and buffeted by ferocious wind.

He managed to get into the bathroom, closed the door and clambered into the old claw foot bathtub. He knew he shouldn't be near a window, but all the destruction was coming from the opposite side of the house. Donovan curled into a ball knowing he could be minutes from death if the howling winds didn't stop. The roaring storm seemed alive, strong enough to pick up the whole house and hurl it into the air.

"God help me!" he cried aloud. He closed his eyes and wondered if this was how his life was going to end. All the time he'd wasted on working and planning out his life was going to be for nothing.

Seconds later, the bathroom ceiling caved in. It felt like he was being crushed by something and he could barely breathe. Were these his last moments on earth? Pain stabbed into his chest and something was crushing his head. He tried to move his hands to shift the thing from his head, but he couldn't move his arms or his hands.

God, if you get me out of this, I'll spend the rest of my life following you.

Silence engulfed him and everything went black.

Chapter Eight

Where am I? Am I dead?

With a huge effort, Donovan opened his eyelids. Bright lights pained his eyes and he closed them.

"Donovan! You're awake."

It was his mother. He was alive. Too weak to speak, he lifted his hand slowly and touched his forehead to feel the fabric of what had to be bandages on his head. The last thing he remembered was the tornado and his house falling in on him.

"You've got some broken ribs, and cuts and bruises, and Dr. Michaels said you also have a severe concussion, which means you have to be still for a few days."

Donovan couldn't move his head, but his eyes opened once more, part way only, to observe his surroundings. He was in a hospital. "Claire?"

His mother leaned over him. "What, dear? Speak up."

"Claire."

"Claire, the maid, was here; I just sent her away. Do

you want her to do something for you? I can do whatever it is."

Donovan moved his eyes to look at his mother. "Claire."

His mother lifted her chin as if she did not approve. "Do you want me to see if she's still here?"

"Yes." His voice was so gravely and raspy, he barely recognized it as his own. He closed his eyes again. It was too much effort to keep them open.

He heard his mother's high heels tapping as she walked out the door. A moment later, he forced his eyelids to open when he felt a comforting hand on his shoulder. Opening his eyes, he saw Claire's smiling face.

"We thought we'd lost you." Claire's voice soothed him.

His mother's voice came from the other side of him. He hadn't known she'd come back in. "If it weren't for Claire's father and brother pulling you out of the rubble, directly after the storm, you might not be here." Her red-rimmed eyes belied her steady voice.

Donovan's mouth turned up at the corners. "Thank you, Claire."

"You get some rest now, Donovan. I'll come back to see you tonight," his mother said.

After he closed his eyes, he heard Claire and his mother say goodbye to each other. Donovan did not know what day it was, and neither did he care. A little corner of his consciousness knew his life would never be the same. He had been granted a second chance and he wasn't going to waste it.

* * *

Later in the evening, Donovan was strong enough to sit up. He learned he didn't have any life-threatening problems, although he had a throbbing headache, and now he wondered how bad the damage was to the house. It had fallen about him, he was sure of it. He recalled half the house had been ripped away and the other half had collapsed on top of him. His mother had mentioned he'd been pulled out of "rubble." Was his whole house destroyed?

An elderly man wearing a long white coat entered his room. Donovan knew it was his doctor. "Hello, I'm Dr. Michaels. You gave us quite a scare, Mr. Billings."

"I'm all right though, aren't I?"

The doctor walked right up to his bedside. "You've got three broken ribs. Broken ribs can be dangerous. You were lucky they didn't pierce any major organs, which is a common complication in this type of break. We can't splint ribs; for one thing, it would limit your breathing and cause further complications." The doctor pulled some X-ray images out of the envelope he was holding. Holding them up to the light, he asked, "Can you see the break?"

Donovan turned away. "I'd rather not look, thanks, Doc."

"You'll need to do some deep breathing exercises to prevent pneumonia; even though it hurts, it's imperative you keep your lungs and ribcage flexible for maximal breathing capacity. Someone from respiratory therapy will be along later to show you those."

"When will I be better?"

"It's hard to say. You'll have to take it easy for a

while. You're young and healthy, but it still takes time. And concussions are pesky, especially if you don't let your brain get enough rest."

Donovan's face twisted into a scowl. "I can't be in here for any length of time."

The elderly doctor frowned right back, and then smiled at him. "You should be able to leave in a day or two, but you'll need to rest. That means absolutely no exertion—and you'll need strong painkillers."

"They've been giving me lots of drugs. Normally, I don't like taking painkillers."

The doctor shook his head. "If you stop taking them, you'll regret it. Trust me. They've got most of the painkillers in your IV for now, but once you leave the hospital, believe me, the pain will get a lot worse. It's going to hurt to breathe, but you must keep stretching out your lungs so use the medication as needed."

A while after the doctor left, Donovan heard his mother's high heels in the corridor. He opened his eyes and watched her come into his room. "You look better," she said when she was by the bed.

"I'm feeling stronger, only it hurts to move. Sharp pains in my sides."

"Yes, that'll be the broken ribs. There's not much anyone can do about them except wait for them to heal."

"I know, the doctor came not long after you left and I heard all about how dangerous broken ribs can be."

"He said there's not any grave danger if you keep still and don't do anything silly."

"Don't worry. I won't be doing anything, not with this pain. It even hurts to take a breath, but I'm still supposed to do breathing exercises. The breaks aren't bad, the doctor tells me, just enough to be painful."

She sat on the chair next to him. "I'm afraid I've got some further bad news."

Donovan looked at his mother and waited for her to continue. How bad could it be? When he saw her bottom lip tremble, he asked, "Is the Porsche all right?"

His mother nodded and her eyes darted away from him. "The Porsche is unharmed. The storm didn't affect the garage at all."

Donovan's immediate reaction was a wave of annoyance with himself for not obeying his first instinct to shelter in the garage. "Well, what's happened? Have I lost Finch House completely?"

"The house, yes...and the restaurant."

He went to sit up straight, but yelled out in pain and had to lie back down.

"I'm sorry, Donovan, I was going to wait until you felt better, but the doctor said you'll be all right to leave the hospital tomorrow or the day after; but only if you have someone to take care of you."

Donovan put his hand to his head.

"I'll look after you at the B&B. I would look after you at my place, but there are always people around at the guest house, so I thought that would be safer."

"Thanks, Mom." After a moment, he asked, "Is the coffee shop okay?"

"The coffee shop's fine."

Donovan's whole body relaxed into the bed and he closed his eyes. He still had the coffee shop, and therefore he still had an income. He opened his eyes and looked at the door.

"She's not here," his mother said.

He frowned at his mother and she gave him a knowing look. She had to know he was looking for Claire. If he said anything, though, it would only lead to a lengthy conversation about something he did not wish to discuss. For some reason, he felt comforted when Claire was near.

When his mother left, it came back to Donovan how he'd called out to God—a God in whom he did not consciously believe. The core of him had to know of the existence of God because his cry to Him had been instinctive. Then he remembered he'd cut God a deal. He sighed. God had saved his life, and he had to keep his part of the bargain.

Donovan couldn't recall his exact words to God, but he knew he had to honor them. He had to follow Him, and change his ways. Closing his eyes, he thought back to when he was curled up in the bathtub knowing he had moments to live. Yes, the promise had been something about finding out more about God and following His ways. Donovan knew he could not go back on his word.

"He's going to be all right then?" Claire's father asked her when she arrived home from visiting Donovan at the hospital.

"*Jah, Dat,* he's fine. He's got broken ribs and a serious knock on the head. The doctor said he'll be okay if he keeps quiet and doesn't exert himself."

"He's lost everything?"

Claire nodded. "*Jah.* Well, no, not everything. You saw his house, and he's lost the restaurant. His mother told me he still has his coffee-shop café in town."

"Ah."

A couple of Amish farms had been affected by the tornado, and her *bruder* and *vadder* had spent the day helping clean up the farms. The community always helped each other when anything happened and they were already planning a barn raising in a week's time for the neighbor who'd lost his barn. That was the worst that had happened to their community—one barn lost.

"It's back to work for me tomorrow," Claire said.

"You'll get to see more of Donovan now that he's laid up sick?"

Claire frowned at Sally and then glanced at her parents. Thankfully, they hadn't taken notice of Sally's question. "Not necessarily."

It was when they were alone in the kitchen doing the after-lunch washing up that Sally said to Claire, "You can't fool me; I know you like that man, the one in the hospital."

"*Jah,* I do, but you can't tell anyone."

"Are you going to leave us then? He's an *Englischer.* If you hadn't noticed already."

Claire shrugged her shoulders; she knew what her *schweschder* meant. Lines formed on Claire's forehead as she wondered why Sally had to be so cruel and meddling. "*Nee,* I'm not going anywhere."

Sally pressed her face a little closer to Claire's, gave her a glare and then walked away. Then she popped her head back into the kitchen. "You do the rest. I'm tired."

Claire knew Sally was annoyed Claire had found a man she was fond of while Sally still had no one. So badly did Sally want to find love that it had made her bitter.

* * *

Claire had the rest of the day to fill, since she didn't have any work. She walked into the family's vegetable garden and set about pulling out weeds from the soft moist soil. She spent the remainder of the day in the garden. In the evening, she helped with dinner and when that was over, she climbed the steps to her room glad Donovan was still alive; he could very easily have died in the storm. Five local people had perished and he could've become the sixth.

Claire pulled off her prayer *kapp* and threw it on her nightstand. Sitting on the end of her bed, she unbraided her hair and brushed it out. She wondered why *Gott* had put Donovan in her path. Was He testing her? From what Jessie had said, Donovan had his share of lady friends and he was not the kind of man who'd be faithful to just one woman. There was no point wasting her time thinking about him. He wouldn't join their community; that would be the last thing in the world a man like Donovan would do.

After she loosely braided her hair into two plaits, she changed into her nightdress and slipped beneath the covers of her bed. She blew out the candle by her bedside and wondered whether all the things Jessie had told her about Donovan were true. She'd have had no reason to lie. *But people can change, can't they?*

Chapter Nine

Claire went to work the next morning and as soon as she arrived Mrs. Billings called her into her office.

"Donovan will be arriving today unless his doctor changes his mind. Anyway, I'd like you to get room three ready for him."

Claire nodded, feeling anxious because she hadn't been shown how to get a room ready.

As though reading her mind, Mrs. Billings said, "Linda will help you and show you what to do. While he's here, you'll be looking after him."

"Me?"

"Yes. Unless that's a problem?" Mrs. Billings looked up at Claire over top of her glasses that perched on the end of her nose.

"No, it's not, not at all." After being given her instructions, Claire went to find Linda.

"Linda, I've got to prepare room three for Donovan. Mrs. Billings said he might be released today."

Linda looked up from making the bed in room two. "Help me out here and we can do number three next."

Claire was relieved Linda was there to help. She knew by what Jessie had told her Mrs. Billings was most particular about everything and she'd be even more so regarding her only child. During their cleaning, Claire told Linda she'd been given the job of looking after Donovan.

Linda straightened up. "I told Jessie this, and I'll tell you; he's no good. He'll break yer heart as soon as look at ya."

"I don't like him in that way; I mean, he seems nice enough, but I'm not interested. No, it's nothing like that." Claire tucked in the corner of the sheet just like she'd been shown.

"It never is." Linda smoothed down the sheet now the ends had been tucked in.

After they had room three ready, Claire reported to Mrs. Billings, "It's all done, Mrs. Billings. What would you have me do now?"

"I've rung the hospital and he'll definitely be out today. I'll drive him back. You help Linda until we arrive."

"Very well." Claire hurried back to Linda, hoping Linda wouldn't warn her again about Donovan. If only there was an Amish man somewhere who could occupy her thoughts as fully. She'd never seriously considered Donovan as a potential boyfriend or husband. He was handsome, charming sometimes, and she could see why Jessie had liked him so much at one point. But now Jessie had Elijah, and both of them were happy.

Claire had heard one report saying the restaurant had escaped damage, but knew that was untrue because Mrs. Billings told her it was ruined. "The restaurant looks all right from the outside," she told Linda as they both looked out the window at it.

"It might look all right, but the whole roof caved in. It's just the walls of the building that are standing," Linda said. "And I hear they're in need of reinforcement."

Donovan's loss was made easier because he had insurance. Hopefully, his insurance covered tornados. His paperwork was at his house and now it was destroyed. He'd phone the insurance company as soon as he got to the guest house. His mother brought him clothes to change into since his own clothes had been cut off him when he was brought to the hospital and the rest were in the ruins of his house. It would be a bit before he'd know what could be salvaged from the house.

"I hope I got your sizes right."

"Anything will do, Mother. I just want to get out of this place and get my life back together."

"I've got Claire looking after you," his mother said.

"No one needs to look after me. I'm not an invalid; I'm perfectly capable of looking after myself."

"She'll be there if you need anything. You know I've got a lot of work to do all the time. I thought you'd be pleased to have your little friend cater to your every need."

"Thank you, Mother; that's good of you."

Donovan pulled on the black trousers his mother had bought him. They were a little loose, but he tightened them with the accompanying belt. He carefully pulled a white tee shirt over his head. His ribs didn't hurt too much if he moved carefully. "Okay, I'm ready." He flung open the curtain by his bed and winced. *Whoa! No sudden moves*, he reminded himself.

His mother looked at his clothes. "The pants are a bit big, and I didn't have the right shirt size, I see. I'll have some clothes delivered for you."

Donovan was wheeled out to Mrs. Billings's car by a hospital worker, then he gingerly lowered himself into his mother's car and they set off.

"Mom, I've been thinking about things while I've been in the hospital. I don't need to work so hard." He studied his mother's face. There was no expression. "I'm considering not re-opening the restaurant, or maybe re-opening it and then selling it."

"I could take it over from you."

He frowned. "In what way?" he asked, wondering why she would take on so many problems at her age.

"I could make half of it into a couple more rooms, and then have a smaller restaurant, just for the patrons of the B&B."

"I guess that would work. Are you sure you want to?"

"I was considering doing that before you opened the restaurant."

He scoffed. "It gives me nothing but problems. The coffee shop's the thing that's going to make me the money, and it's not got all the headaches."

"And where does the maid come into all your new plans?"

"Claire?"

His mother smiled and nodded.

"I like her. I'll admit that. Who wouldn't? I doubt she'd have anything to do with someone like me."

"Quite right. You're way out of her league, and I do

hope she realizes that before you hurt another girl who works for me. I'm counting about three now. Three I know of."

"No, Mother, Claire is way out of *my* league. She's beautiful outside and inside and she's smart." He chuckled. "Smart enough to keep me on my toes, I'd reckon."

Mrs. Billings pursed her collagen-filled lips. "I suppose I owe her and her family gratitude for finding you under all the rubble."

"When I'm able to get around on my own, I'll pay them a visit and thank them properly." After his mother didn't comment, he said, "Mom, do you ever regret not having more children?"

"Donovan, not this again. Will you ever let up?"

"I haven't mentioned anything for years. I just got to thinking if something worse had happened to me, you'd be all alone now; Dad's been gone for years now."

His mother laughed. "People don't have children to keep them company in their old age."

"Some might. It sounds like it could be an advantage. The Amish keep their old folks close to them. They even build on to their houses for their elderly relatives."

"And how would you know?"

"I've had conversations with Claire."

"You always were swayed by a pretty face. There are plenty of other girls you could turn your attention to. You don't want to cause the young girl problems, do you? You do know she has to marry her own kind, don't you? And I don't think her future husband would be happy if you've had your way with her."

"Mother! So crude!"

"I'm telling it like it is. Sometimes you have your head in the clouds and can't see sense."

Donovan was glad when they pulled into the parking lot of the guest house. He opened his door and slowly got out of the car. His mother hovered around trying to help. "I'm all right, Mother, I can walk by myself."

"You're staying in room three. The doctor said you need rest. Get straight into bed. I don't have any pajamas for you yet. I'll get those clothes delivered later today."

"I don't wear pajamas, Mother, and I know I need rest; you keep telling me."

She rolled her eyes. "I'm going to get you pajamas anyway."

Donovan opened the door of number three and climbed into bed. He had one thing on his mind, besides Claire, and that was to phone the insurance company. His phone had survived the storm, and a nurse had returned it to him with the other contents of his pockets. After a lengthy wait on hold, he found out that his insurance covered both the house and the restaurant, but he would have to wait for the insurance assessors due to the large number of claims waiting to be processed. How would his staff get on? He called the insurance company back to see if he had taken out insurance on their behalf for loss of income. The insurance company said the insurance would've had to be taken out by the workers themselves.

Donovan knew his staff wouldn't have paid for income insurance, so he made up his mind he'd keep paying them for as long as he possibly could. The old Donovan wouldn't have done that—wouldn't have even thought of it.

The old Donovan died in the tornado.

He was determined to do things differently. He was thankful he still had the coffee shop, and after he franchised it he could live decently. There was a soft knock on his door. "Come in."

"Hello, Donovan." Claire walked to his bedside. "Your mother's appointed me to look after you."

"Then I'm a lucky man." Claire giggled.

"It's good to see you, Claire. I didn't ask you at the hospital, but was your parents' farm damaged by the storm?"

"No, we escaped it, but two of our neighbor families had their barns destroyed. Well, one of the barns had its roof ripped off, and the other barn was flattened."

"That's awful. And do the Amish believe in insurance?"

Claire shook her head. "It's not necessary; we all help each other when things like this happen. This coming Saturday, we're having a barn raising for the Fullers. They're the ones who lost their barn completely."

"A real Amish barn raising?" Claire nodded.

"Do you think I might be able to watch?"

She smiled. "I don't see why not. Will you be well enough?"

"I'm all right, but I daren't get out of bed for a couple of days with my mother watching over me. She seems to believe I've suffered a bad concussion. I'll be able to make it Saturday."

"Didn't the doctor say you had a concussion?"

He chuckled. "Maybe."

"Why are you interested in a barn raising?"

"I'm interested in all kinds of things. I've never seen

one before, and that's something I'd like to experience. Would you be able to make me a cup of hot tea, Claire?"

"Of course." Claire walked over to the kettle. Each room had tea- and coffee-making facilities and a small fridge. She filled up the kettle and plugged it in.

"I've had a lot of time to think about things, Claire."

Claire spun around. "What things?"

"Life and God." Claire laughed. "What's funny?"

"Oh, you're serious?" Claire put her hand over her mouth. "I'm sorry."

"Of course I'm serious. I'm even thinking of enjoying life for a change. Maybe I won't keep the restaurant. My mother has offered to take it over."

"You'd do that?"

He nodded. "You were right about money not being important. I found that out when I was about to die. I had to ask myself why I had worked so hard. For what? It's not as important as I thought it was."

She heard the kettle boiling, turned and put a teabag in his cup. Neither said a word until she brought his hot tea to him.

"Sit down with me for a moment?" Donovan asked as Claire passed him the teacup.

She pulled up a chair and sat near his bed.

"I had an odd experience when the house was crumbling down around me." He looked at her expectant face. No one he knew would be able to understand, no one but Claire. "I didn't know I believed in God deep down in my heart, but I must've. I called out to Him when I thought I was going to die."

Claire's eyes grew wide. "You did?"

He chuckled. "You don't have to be so shocked."

"No, it's just you seemed to…not believe in Him."

"I suppose I surprised myself. Don't you see, Claire? This is a turning point in my life. It can never be the same. I'm now a believer; I now believe God exists, so with that knowledge, I have to change my ways and I'm going to. I wanted to tell you at the hospital, but Mom was there, and I didn't want to speak of it in front of her." He did not tell Claire he had also promised God a thing or two. That part was between him and God.

Chapter Ten

Donovan pulled up at Claire's house at six o'clock on Saturday morning. After two days in bed, he'd insisted he was well enough to drive and had borrowed his mother's car. His was still in his garage.

Claire came out to greet him. "Hello."

"Hello yourself, jump in."

Claire had had Donovan meet her at her house and then she would take him to the barn raising. Her family had gone on ahead.

"You're sure it's all right that I come?"

"Yes, it is. I asked the Fullers, who own the property, and they said it'll be fine." Claire felt good whenever she was with Donovan, yet she constantly reminded herself she was just one of many girls who had the same feelings for him. She hoped she wouldn't be judged by her friends when they saw her with him.

"I need to thank your brother and your father too. I don't even know what they look like."

"You still remember nothing from when they got to your house?"

"Nothing at all. I only have memory of waking up at the hospital."

Claire nodded. "They'll be working when we get there, but all the men come down and eat. Did I mention there will be a lot of food there? The women are there to prepare the food to have it ready for the men; it's hard work."

A little flicker inside Claire hoped Donovan wanted to see the barn raising because he was slightly interested in the community. Or did he still have feelings for Jessie and he wanted to see her again? He'd mentioned her name once or twice.

Donovan was the kind of man who would not let another man stand in his way. If he liked Jessie, he would find a way to take her away from Elijah, Claire was certain of it. Claire looked at Donovan and he smiled at her.

"You look very pretty today, Claire."

Claire giggled; she was not used to getting compliments. "I look the same every day, I'm sure. Oh, I don't mean the pretty part, but I guess… I never change." Claire frowned at the way she rambled. She didn't want to be prideful, but she did enjoy being able to see what she looked like in the mirrors at the B&B because they had no mirrors at home. She would not call herself pretty or anything of the kind; her reflection told her she was plain.

"You're right; you do look pretty every day."

Claire bit her lip and kept quiet; surely if she opened her mouth again she would say something worse.

The car went over a slight rise.

"It's just here to the left," Claire said.

"Oh, I can see it." When they got away from the trees

lining the property, there was a full view of the barn raising and the lineup of buggies from all of the helpers. "How could they do so much so quickly?"

"They've been here since sunup."

"It's spectacular." Donovan marveled at all the men who appeared as ants running along the new wooden framework of the large structure. He parked his car behind the buggies.

"You go and do what you have to, Claire. Would you normally help the women?"

"Yes. Are you sure you'll be all right?"

"I'll sit over there." Donovan pointed to a log bench under a tree, which was close to the house where the ladies were setting up the food. "I only wish I had a camera."

"You know it wouldn't be allowed, don't you?"

Donovan nodded. "I know."

"If it gets too much for you, let me know. If you feel tired, it might be best to get a taxi and leave your car here."

"I'll be all right. Stop fussing, woman, and go."

Claire smiled at him, then turned and walked toward the ladies.

After half an hour of sitting and watching the spectacle, Donovan saw a tall young man approaching him.

"Hiya."

Donovan slowly rose to his feet hoping it wouldn't hurt his ribs. "Hello, I'm Donovan, a friend of Claire Schoneberger."

The young man smiled widely. "I know, I'm Claire's brother and we've met."

Donovan reached out his hand. "I'm sorry. I remember nothing except waking in a hospital bed. From the bottom of my heart, I thank you. I owe you my life."

While shaking Donovan's hand, the young man said, "I'm Elias Schoneberger. Claire was the one who insisted we see if you were all right. It was just as the storm had gone and we weren't sure if the twister was going to turn and come back."

"Thanks again," Donovan said. "You took a big risk."

"Claire can be persuasive. Sit down," Elias said, and sat on the bench next to his spot.

"This is an amazing sight. I've heard of barn raisings, but I've never seen something like this with my own eyes."

Elias looked toward the half-built barn.

"Tell me, Elias, how can I repay you and your family for what you've done?"

Elias chuckled. "No need to do so, Donovan."

"Is your father here today?"

"Yes, he's here somewhere. I think he's cutting the wood around the back. Are you up for a walk?"

"As long as Claire doesn't see me. She told me to stay here and not go anywhere." He stood up. "Let's go."

Donovan was pleased Elias was so nice and his greeting had been so friendly. He thought Claire's family might be suspicious of an outsider. As they rounded the corner of the frame of the barn, Donovan saw four men cutting wood with handsaws. He was amazed at their speed and precision.

"*Dat*, this is Donovan."

Claire's father leaned his saw against the cutting block.

Donovan and Claire's father shook hands.

"You look a little different." Claire's father chuckled.

"From the bottom of my heart, I thank you for fishing me out of the rubble."

"*Ach,* it was something anyone would do."

"No, you risked your lives to check if I was all right and you didn't even know me. The storm could have turned back on itself."

Claire's father narrowed his blue eyes. "I've learned women know things sometimes. Claire insisted, and I had to listen."

Donovan felt the back of his eyes sting, and he blinked a couple of times. "Thank you." He did not ask if he could do anything for the family in case it wasn't met with a good response. He had quickly learned he had nothing, neither could he buy anything for them they would want. Donovan looked up at the barn. "This is truly something to see."

"We all work together to help each other." Mr. Schoneberger took his hat off and scratched his head.

"I'll go back to my seat and keep watching." Donovan gave the men a nod, and then walked away from Claire's brother and father. Before he got back to his bench under the tree, he came across Elijah, Jessie's boyfriend. "Hello, Elijah."

Elijah tipped his head. "Donovan."

"I might have building work for you and Henry soon. My restaurant was destroyed by the storm, so was my house, unfortunately. Anyway, I might phone your uncle soon."

"I'm sorry to hear it. Do you want us to come by and give a quote?" Elijah asked.

"Soon. I'm waiting on the insurance assessors to have a look at it first. Anyway, I won't keep you; everyone looks busy."

Elijah nodded, and they went separate ways.

Donovan sat back on his bench seat. Jessie had been right to choose Elijah over him. And if things had worked out between himself and Jessie, he might not have gotten to know Claire.

"Coffee?"

Donovan drew his eyes from the barn, turned and fixed his gaze upon Claire, who approached him from behind. "How did you know?"

"I know you like three coffees every morning, and you probably didn't have time for any this morning, did you?"

"No. Can you sit awhile, or are you needed back there?"

She sat down next to him. "I can stay."

He sipped his coffee. "Mmm, there's nothing like fresh coffee in the morning."

They sat quietly and watched the men run over the barn like ants.

"I found your father and your brother. Well, your brother found me, and took me to your father. I thanked them."

She raised her eyebrows. "You did? What did they say to you?"

"Claire, you shouldn't have put your family in danger, sending them to check I was all right. Elias told me the storm could've turned back. The winds were strong enough to heave cows through the air, so I don't think your buggy would've handled it too well. You shouldn't have put yourself and your family in danger just for me."

"It was something I had to do. I just knew you were in some kind of trouble. I could feel it."

"Never do anything like that again, Claire. I'd rather get badly hurt than you risk yourself or your family." He took another sip of coffee. "I've learned the community has no insurance, and they don't need it because you all help each other. This barn raising is a testament to it."

Claire nodded. "It's just the way it is. We're a big family and families help their members."

"Must be comforting." He looked into Claire's eyes and she smiled at him. He wanted to ask what he needed to do for them to be a real couple, but he didn't want to scare her away. He wanted to be able to hold her in his arms and protect her. He knew it had only been days since he'd met her, but she was the woman for him. He had an inkling she might've felt the same way.

"Claire, are you helping or what?"

Claire swung her head around, and Donovan turned carefully to see a short thickset woman who looked a little like Claire.

"Is that your mother?" he whispered.

Claire gave a slight shake of her head and whispered back, "Sister."

The sister walked closer. "You've hardly done a thing."

"Sally, this is Donovan."

Her lips turned up at the corners, but this woman still had her knuckles firmly planted on her hips. "Hello, Donovan."

Donovan stood slowly. "Nice to meet you, Sally."

Claire jumped to her feet. "I'll bring you back some food when the meal is ready, Donovan." She hurried away with her sister.

"So that's Donovan?" Sally asked as they walked away from him.

"Yes, and you didn't have to be so rude to him. And I have been helping."

"I wasn't rude. I just don't know why you came here if you're not going to work."

"I just took him coffee, that's all."

"You were sitting talking to him, and I noticed his coffee was nearly all gone, and that's the truth. You must have been speaking to him for a time instead of helping us."

Claire rubbed the back of her neck. Why did her *schweschder* think it necessary to check on her all the day long?

Just as they neared the food preparation annex, Sally said, "He seems nice."

Claire turned to her with raised brows. "You think so?"

Sally nodded. "For an *Englischer*."

Half an hour later, Claire was mixing the dressing into the potato salad when Jessie pulled on her arm. "Claire, Elijah told me you brought Donovan here."

"*Jah,* he wanted to see a barn raising."

Jessie's eyes opened wide. "What about all those things I told you about him?"

"Do you know he's been very ill? He's got broken

ribs, and his house fell down around him, and he's only just gotten out of the hospital."

"*Jah,* your *mudder* told my *mudder.*" Jessie frowned at Claire.

"I know all the things you said about him, but people can change," Claire said.

Jessie leaned forward, and whispered, *"Can a leopard truly change his spots? Though thou shouldest bray a fool in a mortar among wheat with a pestle, yet will not his foolishness depart from him."*

Chills ran through Claire's body. She knew the first quote was from Jeremiah in the Bible, and the second was a scripture from Proverbs, which she guessed meant the same thing. Maybe she was wrong about Donovan changing, and *Gott* might be telling her so through Jessie. Claire looked into her concerned friend's face and nodded.

Jessie continued, "*Ach,* Claire, I know he can say nice things and he'll make you feel like you're the only woman in the world, but I don't think he's a faithful man, and he's not got our morals."

Claire pulled a face. A good dose of reality was just what she'd needed. Her heart had begun to open to Donovan, and now she had to close it—tight.

Chapter Eleven

As she'd said she would, Claire took a plate of food over to Donovan. By that time, some of the men were speaking with him, so she did not have to talk to him at all. She wondered what the men had been saying, as they all stopped speaking when she approached. When she had handed Donovan the plate, she went directly back to helping the women.

A while later, she saw Donovan approaching the meal annex. She went to meet him, aware people were watching them.

"Thanks for letting me come here today, Claire. I'll go now. Did you want me to drive you home?"

"No, thank you, I'll go home in the buggy with my parents. We'll be here 'til sundown."

Claire watched Donovan walk away. He was not back to his old self. His walk was slow and deliberate, the walk of someone in a great deal of pain. She turned away from him determined to put him out of her mind. She would not see him until Monday. Surely, she could stop thinking about him for one whole day tomorrow, and the half of today that remained.

As Donovan drove away from the crowd, he had a sense of peace like he'd never known. There was a quiet and a calm amongst the Amish folk.

He wondered whether a girl like Claire would ever be interested in a man such as he. Even though he knew he could join them if he wanted, he'd never live a backward life with no technology. He saw no sense in living without electricity and basic necessities—as he saw them—to be right in God's sight.

The next day was Sunday, and since there was no gathering, Claire set out to visit Olive. Sunday was a *gut* day to visit others. Since Claire could not get Donovan out of her mind, she decided Olive was the best choice. Olive had fallen in love with a man who'd joined the community, so maybe she could offer advice on *Englischers*.

"Olive, I need to speak to you privately."

"Okay." Olive nodded. "Let's go for a walk."

They headed off down the driveway to walk along the roadside.

"What is it, Claire? You look troubled."

"I like a boy. I should say, a man."

"Donovan, the *Englischer* who was at the barn raising?"

Claire nodded. "*Jah*, and it's the same one Jessie used to like. She said terrible things about him, but I think he's changed."

"He might have changed, but he's not Amish."

"That's what I wanted to talk to you about. Blake joined the community and you'll be married to him soon. How did it come about?"

Olive looked down at the ground. "He had believed in God for a while. He was willing to join the community. It's nothing I did or said to force him."

"*Nee*, I didn't think you would have forced him. I just thought you might have some advice for me. I think I'm in love; I can't stop thinking of him. It worries me."

Olive's eyes fixed upon Claire's, and Olive stopped still. "I don't have any advice, Claire, except to pray about it and leave it for *Gott* to work out. If it is meant to be, he will join us, and if not, then someone else will come along for you."

Claire scratched her neck and screwed up her nose. "Do you really believe that?"

"*Jah,* I do."

Something told Claire that Donovan would never join the community. He just wouldn't. She would have to find a way to rid him from her mind. Maybe she should not return to her job. No, she had to stay and make sure he was all right. At least she would stay until he was completely healthy and back on his feet. Besides, she had told his mother she'd stay for at least a year.

"Have you spoken to the other girls about this?"

Claire knew she meant their other three friends, Amy, Jessie and Lucy. "*Nee,* I don't want them to know. I have spoken to Jessie. I mean, she's warned me about him, but she doesn't know I like him. I think she has an idea I might like him from what she said. I guess by now they've all heard he was at the barn raising, but they haven't mentioned it to me."

"I won't say anything, then."

"*Denke*, Olive. I just thought you would be the one who might have some advice for me."

"I guess you just have to wait and see how things turn out."

Claire nodded. "Now, how are things with you?"

"Couldn't be better. Blake is learning about the community and Leo has all the Hilty *kinner* to play with." Olive was speaking of the Hilty family Blake was staying with before he officially joined them.

"When does Blake take the instructions?"

"He's doing them now."

"Good. Do you get to spend much time with them?"

"I see them almost every other day, but we're never alone. I guess we have to wait 'til we're married to be properly alone. He said he's been looking for a *haus* for us to live in, but he hasn't found one yet. He has a funny smile on his face when he talks about it, so I think he's got something he's not telling me."

"Maybe he wants to surprise you."

Olive nodded. "That's what I think."

The mention of Olive soon having a home of her own set Claire's thoughts in the direction of Donovan's house and how it'd been flattened. Then she was annoyed with herself for continually thinking about him.

Back in the guest house and in bed since his return from yesterday's barn raising, Donovan flicked the buttons of the TV remote trying to find something to watch. He would have to last the day without seeing Claire again. When his phone rang, he looked at the caller I.D. to see it was one of the casual girlfriends he used to date. He pressed "cancel" and then went through his phone and deleted several girls' phone numbers. When he finished, he went through his phone again and deleted photos and texts. He was no longer interested in any of them.

He threw his phone onto the chair next to the bed. How could he make Claire be interested in him? She would not be swayed by expensive gifts, and neither could he whisk her away to Paris for a weekend. She was one woman he couldn't let slip away from him. If he had to change himself to win her heart then he'd do it.

Claire was good and kind, but she was also smart, and she was someone who would not put up with his nonsense. He smiled as he remembered how it felt to be near her. Donovan considered driving to see her, but what excuse would he give for doing so? He couldn't say he missed her serene face and quiet voice. Would Claire be scared away forever if she knew his true feelings? He was sure he was in love. He had never had these feelings for any other woman. With Jessie, the feelings had never been this intense, this deep.

He had to be honest and tell Claire about his feelings for her. But tomorrow was a long way away. Donovan looked at his watch to see it was just past the hour. Hopefully, there would be some different shows on TV.

"Lunch?" His mother poked her head around the door.

"Yes, thanks, Mom." Conveniently, his mother lived next door to the guest house.

"I've got some soup coming for you." She sat on the end of his bed. "What are you watching?"

"Nothing, just trying to find something interesting to pass the time, but there's nothing."

"Do you want me to bring some books or some magazines?"

Donovan sighed. "No. You could pass my laptop over."

"No. No work, you need to rest and relax."

Donovan's mouth fell open. He wasn't used to hearing the word "no." "I will be resting. I'm not going to exert myself by pressing a few buttons."

"No, but you'll see an email or something that'll cause you stress. Stress is a killer, and it'll make your body take longer to heal."

He shook his head. "Mom, you sound like you've been listening to some New Age guru."

Mrs. Billings wagged her finger in her son's face. "It's plain common sense and it's something you sometimes lack. You've got to look after your health."

"Thanks, Mother."

"I mean it."

"You're the one stressing me, Mother."

Mrs. Billings chuckled. "Why don't you and I go out somewhere nice for dinner tonight? Are you up to it?"

"Thanks, I am, and it would be good to have a change of scene."

"I'll bring your soup." Mrs. Billings left him alone and brought the soup back a quarter of an hour later.

When he'd finished the soup, he looked at his watch to see it was two in the afternoon. It had been a long time since he'd gone out with his mother. He reached out to the bedside chest, popped two painkillers in his mouth, took a gulp of water and swallowed the pills.

He hoped he would not get into an argument with his mother over dinner. He closed his eyes and dozed, knowing his mother would wake him if he slept too long.

That evening, while eating his dinner, Donovan told his mother about the barn raising.

"So, it was a real barn raising like you see on TV?" she asked.

"Yes, it was a real one, not a fake one."

His mother chuckled. "You're just like your father. What was it like?"

"It was quite remarkable. The barn went up at lightning speed. There were dozens of workers and they each knew what they had to do and no one got in anyone's way." He rubbed his eyebrows. "Remarkable," he repeated.

"I suppose Claire was delighted you went?"

"I suppose she was." He looked his mother in the eyes. "I like her, Mom. I really do."

"You like all of them, Donovan." She piled some of her vegetarian risotto onto her fork and daintily placed it into her mouth.

Donovan looked up from his steak. "No, that's in the past. From now on, I'm a changed man."

His mother giggled as though he'd said something hilarious. "And what brought about this change?"

"I've had time to think in the hospital. I've thought about life and about God."

She loaded more risotto onto her fork. "And what have you decided?"

"I'm serious, Mom."

Mrs. Billings placed her still-loaded fork down onto her plate. "I've never heard you speak like this."

"That's because I've never given much thought to life and the meaning of it." He popped a portion of steak into his mouth and chewed thoughtfully. "Being nearly dead has caused me to view things differently."

His mother took a sip of wine and then said, "Your father believed in God—if that's where this conversation is headed."

"He did? You never told me that."

Mrs. Billings shrugged her shoulders. "I didn't think it was important."

"Did you ever believe?"

"I believe in science."

"Yes, but can't science and God coexist? Wouldn't God have put science in place?" He cut another piece of steak and placed it in his mouth.

His mother waved a hand in the air. "I've never bothered to give it too much thought. I'd rather think on more practical things."

Donovan knew it was no good talking to his mother of such things when he wasn't sure of what he believed except in the existence of a divine creator. He finished chewing his mouthful then sighed loudly. "I've been thinking about these things. That's what nearly dying does to a person."

"You do need a nice girl. That's what I've wanted for you for a long time, but please, not an Amish girl. You go from one extreme to the other. It's because you're slightly hyperactive, or whatever the term is for it these days." Mrs. Billings rolled her eyes, and then patted his hand. "You'll get over her."

He smiled at his mother and had no idea what she meant.

Chapter Twelve

Donovan woke early Monday morning pleased he'd see Claire. He had a shower, got dressed and then lay on his bed waiting for her to arrive. Just after nine o'clock, there was a gentle knock on his door. "Come in." He held his breath, hoping.

Claire pushed the door open and stepped through. "How are you today?"

He smiled. She was even more beautiful than he remembered. "I'm fine. I do have an appointment back at the hospital at eleven. They need to do another brain scan, or some test or other."

"Do you want me to come with you?"

"Yes. Could you? Of course, you can. I'll clear it with my mother."

"Have you had breakfast?" Claire asked.

He shook his head and wondered why his mother hadn't been in with his breakfast.

"I'll get you some."

"Please, just toast and coffee." Claire nodded and left his room.

How would he tell Claire of his feelings? Could he just come straight out and say something? He ground his teeth and considered how to bring something like that up in conversation. This was something he'd never been concerned with before Claire came into his life.

His door opened. "I just met your mother with the breakfast tray. She said she'd be in later to see you."

"Good. Did you tell her of the eleven o'clock appointment?"

"I did."

Claire placed the breakfast tray across his stomach. "Ow."

"Oh, no. I'm sorry I forgot about your ribs."

He grimaced with the pain. "Just sit by me and pass the food to me."

Claire sat next to him and took the lid off the food. "You have French toast by the looks."

"Oh, good. That's much better than plain toast."

Claire cut off part of the French toast, loaded the fork with a bite and handed it to him along with the cup of maple syrup for dipping.

When he had finished his first mouthful, he said, "What did you do yesterday?"

Claire looked down at the food and continued to cut. "I visited some friends."

"No church?"

"We only have the gatherings every other Sunday."

"I see."

"Sunday is always a day of rest, so no one works on Sunday. Even our food for the day is prepared ahead of time to give the women rest."

"Ah, and it's always the women who cook?"

"Mostly, yes. The men do the outside work. Except the women usually do the gardening and sometimes look after the smaller animals, like the chickens and pigs. There are no absolute rules of who does what."

"Sounds like every day is mapped out for you."

Claire nodded, and handed him his fork loaded with French toast.

"Claire, what would it take for a woman such as you to like a man like me?"

She swallowed hard. "I do like you, Donovan."

"No, not like that. I mean, what would it take for you to have a real relationship with me?"

Her cheeks flushed with color and her eyes grew wide. "It wouldn't work. It simply couldn't."

He was certain Claire liked him. Years of being in business had helped him to read people to a certain extent. "You would like it to work, wouldn't you?" He moved slightly then grimaced again with the pain from his fractured ribs.

Her hand flew to his arm. "Careful."

"Tell me this, if I were Amish would you go on a date with me?"

"You're not Amish, Donovan, so there's no point in me answering." She cut the rest of his toast into bite-sized pieces, left them within his reach on the side of the bed and then stood up. "Now, finish your toast and drink your coffee, and I'll be back a little before ten-thirty."

She placed the coffee mug in his hands and left the room. His head pushed back into the pillow. Where had he gone wrong? He slurped his coffee between bites of food, not even caring it was all lukewarm.

* * *

After the appointment at the hospital, Donovan stopped his car at a park not far from the town center. "Claire, I can't go back and lay around in bed all day like an invalid. Let's sit in the park."

Claire agreed and they walked around the park until they came to a seat overlooking a duck pond.

They both sat, and Donovan slid forward a little and turned his body to face Claire. "I don't know how to do this because I've never had to ask a girl this question before. Girls used to gravitate toward me, and well, things just happened and that's why I find it hard to say what I'm about to say."

Her nose crinkled. "Well, just say it."

"I would like you to be my girlfriend."

Claire jumped up. "I can't."

"Claire, sit down. Talk to me. Why do you say you can't?" He took hold of her hand and gently pulled her back down next to him. "Is it because you don't like me in that way?"

"You're not Amish and it would never be allowed."

"What if you left?" He tilted his head to one side. He knew it was not a question of how she felt regarding him; it was clear they were meant for each other. She had to feel the same.

She looked up at the sky. "I couldn't leave my *familye*."

He still had hold of her hand, and he gave it a squeeze. "You could create a new family—together with me."

She pulled her hand away from his.

He leaned back on the seat. "Claire, no matter what

you heard about me, I can promise I'm a changed man. What's more, I believe in God."

"But you're not Amish."

"What does it matter? I believe in God. Why do I have to go without electricity and a basic standard of living just to prove it? It makes no sense."

Claire stood up again. "What's wrong with our standard of living?"

"I'm not insulting you." He pulled Claire down again. "Claire, I don't want to argue about electricity and buggies and things. I believe in the one true God. Isn't that enough—that we both believe?"

She put her hands over her face. Then her hands lowered as she looked at him. "Donovan, why do things have to be so hard?"

He chuckled. "They're not hard. I want you to be my girl and if I have to marry you to show you I'm serious, I'm willing to do so. I will."

Her eyebrows rose. "You want to marry me?"

He looked up to the sky. "My mother always said I rush into things, but so far everything I've rushed into has always been right. Well, maybe not so much the restaurant, but I knew that one was a gamble from the start." He turned to her and took her hand. "Will you marry me, Claire?"

Tears fell down Claire's face. She stood up and said, "I can't; I just can't."

He stood up and faced her, ignoring the pain pinching at his side. "Shh, don't cry. I understand. I'm not going anywhere. I'm going to be here when you change your mind, waiting for you."

She wiped her tears away and smiled at him. "Blake

joined the community. It's not a hard thing to do. You see, you don't need to lose what you've got. He's working things out with the bishop so he can still have his business. You don't need to give everything away to join us."

"I see. That's interesting. I thought... Well, even though you say that, I still couldn't live cut off from society. The only society I've ever known. I'm sorry, Claire, I just couldn't. But, if you leave, we can have a similar life together. It would be easier for both of us. You can do whatever you like when you're my wife. You can work or not work—anything."

"I'm sorry. I can't leave everything I've ever known either, just for love."

"You love me?"

She looked down at the ground. "I can't say more."

"I understand." Donovan looked at his watch. "I'll drive you home. Not much use going back to the B&B this late in the day."

Hoping her eyes weren't red, Claire walked toward the house. She could already see Sally looking out the kitchen window at her. No doubt, Sally would have something to say about Donovan driving her home, again.

Claire pushed open the back door and was immediately faced with Sally.

"What was *he* doing driving you home?"

"I went to the hospital with him for a checkup."

"Humph." Sally stood with her solid frame square in front of Claire, so Claire could not get past her. "Why are your eyes red?"

"I don't know. They've been a bit sore all day. I think I've got an allergic reaction to something."

"Or, someone." Sally stared at her some more. "Well, you can help with dinner now you're here."

Claire joined her *mudder* in the kitchen. All she wanted was to be alone, but she had to wait until after dinner and it was only mid-afternoon.

After dinner, Claire was finally in the privacy of her bedroom and her thoughts turned to Donovan. How could things possibly work between them? There was no support amongst their families at all. Mrs. Billings looked down her nose at her, and her *familye* would never accept an *Englischer*. They'd be isolated and alone.

If she did leave the community, she wouldn't be shunned because she had not been baptized and therefore was not an official member. Only official members could be shunned, but her *familye* could very well choose not to associate with her. She knew of many families who did not speak with family members who'd left the community.

Why was everything so difficult? She sat sideways on her windowsill and looked toward the setting sun. The sky turned from orange into pink and lavender, gradually darkening as the sun finally sank behind the distant trees.

Donovan said he'd changed. She'd never seen the side of him she'd been warned about. She'd seen his temper on the first day, but it was the only negative thing she could recall. If Jessie was right in the things she said about Donovan, he had gone from being a womanizer to a man who believed in God and wanted to settle with one woman. No, not just "one woman," he wanted to marry her.

Claire sighed and threw herself onto her bed. He'd changed, he had made a huge change and she'd stayed the same. Should she, or could she, compromise a little in order to have love in her life? He'd wanted to meet her halfway; should she take one step and meet him in the middle?

"*Gott,* I have no idea what's right and what's wrong anymore. I love Donovan and want to be with him, but don't know how it would ever work. I give the problem to you to sort out." Claire spoke softly to *Gott.* Now she would have to leave things in His hands and know the outcome would be His will.

She pushed Donovan out of her mind the best she could and went downstairs to see what her *familye* were doing. Sometimes at night they played board games or Dutch Blitz and right now, she needed a distraction.

Chapter Thirteen

That night, as Donovan again flicked through the TV stations trying to find something to watch, his thoughts returned to Claire. He knew things would eventually work out between them. He would have to be patient and not turn back to his wicked ways. He knew if he did so he would surely lose her forever. If he'd been convinced the Amish way was the only true way he'd seriously consider joining them. He had no such evidence it was so. If he joined the community solely to marry Claire he'd probably not be the only man to do such a thing, but he'd be a hypocrite. *And could I be happy in the Amish community?*

The idea of living such a restricted life was not something he wished to ponder, so he didn't consider it for any length of time. How long would it take Claire to realize they belonged together?

Flashes of being crushed under the roof popped into Donovan's mind, and he remembered he told God he would get to know Him. His love for Claire had distracted him from doing so up until now. He stood up from his bed and looked through the three drawers of the nightstand until he found a Bible. For some reason, his mother had one in every room. Probably a leftover habit from when his parents had owned the hotels. There had always been a Gideon Bible in every one of those rooms.

Okay, I said I would get to know God and I guess this is the best way.

He opened the Bible and it fell open at The Psalms. He read for two hours before he fell asleep with the Bible across his chest.

When Claire woke, all she could think about was Donovan. These days he was rarely out of her mind. She couldn't wait to see him and decided she wanted to marry him more than anything. If only she could make him understand life in the community was good. After she decided to go to work early, she replaced her nightgown with her pale yellow dress and pulled on her over-apron.

I must convince him he can live in the community and be happy.

Claire placed the final pin in her hair. She pulled her prayer *kapp* on and tied it under her chin. The smell of baking bread wafted up to her room. Sally was the one who baked the family's bread, and Sally would have something to say about her going to work so early. Claire decided to slip out of the house before Sally saw her and without eating breakfast.

She got to the barn, successfully unnoticed, and wheeled out her bicycle. As soon as Claire had one leg over, she looked up to see her *schweschder* scowling at her from the kitchen window. Claire smiled and waved as she rode away.

Claire knew she didn't want to end up with a bitter heart like Sally had developed. What good was it to stay in the community alone and miserable? If she gave up the chance to marry Donovan, she would risk "catching" Sally's unhappy disposition. She'd have to live with Sally in the family home, and her own mood would surely turn sour too. It was no way to live.

She knew in her heart if all those stories about Donovan had been true, he'd changed. The Donovan she knew would never do such things, and now he professed to believe in *Gott*. Claire smiled and pushed harder on the pedals.

She arrived in Donovan's room breathless, with her face flushed.

He was asleep when she softly opened his door. She sat next to him figuring she would wait silently 'til he woke. She saw a Bible lying across his chest and was delighted he'd been reading it, but hoped it wasn't hurting his ribs. She stood up and gently moved it away.

As soon as she sat down again, he opened one eye. "Claire." He tried to sit up too quickly and winced with the pain.

"Where's your medication?"

"No, I don't need pills. I just moved too fast." He smiled and put out his hand and she put her hand in his. "Are you early?"

"Yes."

"And you're out of breath?"

"Yes."

They both laughed. She wanted to tell him she loved

him and wanted to marry him, but words escaped her as she looked into his kind eyes.

He gently lifted one eyebrow. "Have you reconsidered my question?"

She licked her lips. Now was her opportunity to tell him how life really was in the community. "Donovan, I want you to know your life wouldn't have to change so much if you joined the community."

"Go on."

"Many Amish folk own businesses. They own building companies, B&Bs, restaurants, food marts, furniture and craft stores, and all kinds of things."

He rubbed his chin.

She continued, "The bishop also allows electricity and computers in places of business." Claire lowered her voice, "Just not in the home."

"Is that so?"

Claire nodded. "It's not so bad to live without electricity. I mean, I guess the light is not as strong, but it's softer and more romantic. And we do have plumbing—indoors, even." She giggled. "And cooking can just as easily be done with gas. In fact, many people prefer to cook with gas."

Donovan smiled and looked down at her hand he held. "Come closer."

She leaned in toward him.

"Let's set all that aside for one moment. Whether we live Amish or not, will you answer me one question?"

Claire's eyes grew wide while she waited for him to continue.

"Do you, Claire Schoneberger, love me?"

She looked at his lips and everything within her was

compelled to kiss him, but modesty held her back. "Yes, Donovan Billings, I do." It was a relief to be so open and honest.

"Then marry me and I'll give you my word I will look into joining the Amish community. I can't promise I will, but I'll find out all I can and make a decision."

Her gaze fell away from him. He was not giving her a proper answer. She wanted to hear he'd join, just like Blake had. Didn't he love her enough?

"Claire." She looked back into his eyes and badly wanted to say she'd marry him. "You do love me, don't you?" he asked.

She nodded. "Yes, I do."

"Then marry me and trust everything will work out how it's meant to."

She thought once more about Sally, whose life was wasting away, and also her chances of having children were lessening with each passing day. Claire wanted to have children while she was young and have many of them. Life would pass too quickly waiting for an Amish version of Donovan. If she said no to Donovan, what if no one ever came for her? Closing her eyes for a moment, she further assessed the situation. Here was a man in front of her offering happiness, a life and a family. He was sincere about believing in God, so he wasn't a heathen—an unbeliever. Something inside told her to seize the chance. When she opened her eyes, a smile spread across her face. "Yes, Donovan, yes."

"Come here." He opened his arms and she very gently embraced him. "Let's get married as soon as we can and we can decide about the rest of our lives after we're married. Whether we live in the community or not," he said. "We'll decide together."

Claire bit her lip. "Where will we live?"

"We could stay here for a while."

"Your mother won't think I'm suitable for you."

"Nonsense, 'whatever makes you happy,' is what my mother will say. Then we can rebuild my house and live there. What do you say?"

Claire nodded. "Okay."

"We'll get a marriage license today and get married as soon as we can. As soon as we marry, we'll lease a house while we wait on the rebuilding of Finch House. What do you think about you staying here now, once we tell your family we're getting married?"

Claire covered her mouth and looked away from him. "Claire, I'm not suggesting anything other than separate rooms. I've enough money to pay my mother for our rooms and I've got a lot more money coming from insurance."

Claire managed a smile. "I've never lived away from home."

"Your new home is with me. I keep my word, Claire. I'm not just saying I will look into joining the community to keep you happy. I mean it, I will." He threw the covers off him. "Let's tell your parents right now."

Claire giggled. "Right now?"

"Right now. You step outside and I'll get changed."

She nibbled on the end of a fingernail hoping her folks wouldn't be too upset. "My father will be working on the farm somewhere at this time."

"Then we'll find him and tell him." Donovan shooed her out of the room.

Claire left his room and walked to the kitchen of the B&B to get herself a glass of water. Everything was happening so fast her head was spinning.

Claire's father and her brother, Elias, were mending a fence on the far side of the property. She'd spotted them from Donovan's car. He parked and then they walked toward them.

"Is it polite I ask your father for your hand?" Donovan whispered to Claire.

"No, it's not done. No one asks."

Elias was the first to see them. He tapped his father on the shoulder and his father turned around and waited for Claire and Donovan to reach them. Elias and Mr. Schoneberger nodded hello to Donovan and then looked at Claire.

"The reason we've come to find you is to tell you Claire has agreed to marry me."

"Ach," her father said as he took off his hat. "Is this what you want, Claire?"

"Jah, Dat, more than anything."

Her father nodded and looked at Donovan.

"You would marry an *Englischer,* Claire, and leave us?" Elias asked.

Claire looked up into Elias's face.

Donovan spoke before Claire had a chance. "I would like to learn more about the community. I have told Claire I will seriously consider joining, if I'm welcome, of course. I need to make an informed decision. Claire has agreed to marry me either way."

"Are you angry, *Dat?"* Claire bit her lip not knowing

if she could go through with it without their approval, and what if her mother cried?

"*Nee*, I thought this would happen when I saw Donovan at the barn raising. You're not the only one who sometimes knows things. Have you told your *mudder?*"

"*Nee*, we're going to do that now."

Her father nodded solemnly. "I'll come with you."

Donovan and Claire drove in the car and arrived at the house first. Staying in the car, they talked while they waited for Claire's father and Elias to arrive.

"Your father took it better than I expected."

"He's always been that way," Claire said. "He has a lot of faith."

Donovan nodded.

Claire and Donovan got out of the car once Elias and Mr. Schoneberger arrived and they all walked into the house together.

Claire saw her mother coming out of the kitchen wiping her hands on a dishtowel. "Is anything wrong?"

Sally appeared behind their mother, standing with her arms crossed in front of her chest.

Dat spoke first. "Claire has something to tell you."

Claire took a deep breath. She hadn't known how hard this was going to be. "*Mamm,* Donovan and I are getting married."

She blinked a couple of times. "Your *vadder* and I thought this might happen. Are you leaving the community?"

Claire looked at Donovan, who stood next to her, and he gave her a smile. "For a time; Donovan might join us later."

Donovan gently gave her a nudge with his shoulder,

prompting her to say, "I'll collect my things and go now. I'll be staying at the bed and breakfast."

"Ah, separate rooms, of course," Donovan added, "until the wedding."

Her *mudder* took a deep breath and looked at her husband. Claire's *vadder* put his arm around her *mudder*.

"I'll help you pack your clothes," Sally said softly.

Sally walked ahead of Claire up the stairs. Once they were inside Claire's room, Sally said, "I'm pleased for you, Claire."

"You are?"

"*Jah,* I would do the exact same thing if I ever found anyone to love."

Claire spun around toward Sally and gave her a hug. She had approval from one member of her family, and it was the last person she'd expected. "*Denke,* Sally."

"You're welcome, little *schweschder.*"

After they had packed some things into a large bag, Claire walked down the stairs.

"You'll come back and visit us?" her *mudder* asked with tears in her eyes.

"*Jah,* I will, *Mamm.* Don't cry, please don't."

Her mother nodded, and Claire was pleased they weren't going to cut her off.

Claire hugged everyone goodbye and then Donovan and she drove away.

"Is that how you expected things to be?" Donovan asked.

Claire wiped tears from her eyes. "They took the news better than I thought they would. Sally even said she was happy for me. It's the hardest thing I ever had to do."

Donovan raised his eyebrows and grabbed her hand. "I'll always be here for you. Now to tell my mother."

"How will you do that?"

"Very quickly." Donovan laughed.

Claire looked out the window as they drove away from the only place she'd ever called home. She knew she would have to leave the past behind in order to create something new.

They arrived at the B&B to see Mrs. Billings's car was in the driveway.

"She's here. Come on, let's go tell her," Donovan said.

Claire nodded and tried to smile at him, but her insides gnawed at her.

When they walked in, Mrs. Billings was sitting at the reception desk. "Hello, Mom, where's Yvonne?"

"Everyone needs a day off, Donovan."

"Ah."

Mrs. Billings looked at Claire and it was obvious she was wondering why they were together.

"Mom, there's only one way I can say this, and that is to say it quickly."

She narrowed her eyes at her son.

"This beautiful lady right here has agreed to marry me."

Mrs. Billings sprang up from her chair. "Really?"

"Yes," Donovan said. "And we're going to get married as soon as we possibly can."

Claire knew exactly what she was thinking. "I guess it is a little fast."

"It's not! I was engaged to Donovan's father a week after we met. It was on our first date when he asked me to marry him. I said yes. This is history repeating itself." She walked around the reception desk and hugged Donovan and then hugged Claire. "I'm happy for you both and happy for me. I have a wedding to plan."

"No, Mom. We don't want any fuss." He turned to Claire. "Do we?"

She shook her head.

Donovan continued, "No, we don't want a fuss. We'll have a small ceremony and that's all we want. No engagement party, no other kinds of parties, nothing."

Mrs. Billings's hands flew to her mouth. When she removed them, she said, "I'll finally have grandchildren."

Donovan sneered. "Mom, you hate children."

"No, I don't." She glared at Donovan.

"Whatever you say. I won't argue. I hope you've got an extra couple of rooms for the next few months. Claire and I are staying here, in separate rooms for now. I'll pay of course. We'll be here until we get married; then I'll lease a house. Then we'll move into Finch House when it's been rebuilt."

Mrs. Billings looked at Claire. "Are you leaving your community, Claire?"

Claire opened her mouth to speak, but Donovan spoke for her. "That's a long story, Mom, and right now, Claire and I are going out for a bite to eat. It's been an intense morning." He guided Claire to the doorway. "Oh, and, Mom…"

"Yes?"

"Claire quits."

"Of course," Mrs. Billings said before she sat down. Claire pulled on Donovan's arm. "No, wait. I need to do something, and besides, I gave your mother my word I'd stay a year."

Mrs. Billings called out, "That's quite all right, Claire. We can sort it out when Donovan's not around."

Claire and Donovan looked at each other and laughed. "That wasn't so bad, was it?" he whispered, once they were outside.

"No, it wasn't."

He put his arms around Claire. "We'll have a good life together, you and I."

Claire buried her head into his shoulder and in the safety of his strong arms she knew everything would work out well. "I know we will, Donovan, I just know it." She was comforted by Mrs. Billings's reaction. It was important to have family support. The next thing would be to tell her girlfriends. She hoped they'd take the news well and wouldn't be cross with her. In particular, she wondered about Jessie's reaction since she'd already warned her about Donovan.

Chapter Fourteen

Claire had asked the girls to meet her at the Coffee House, their usual gathering place for every other Saturday—when they could. They hadn't met there for months now, due to most of them having jobs, and sometimes having to work that day. Claire had been in touch with them all, wanting the five of them face-to-face to break the news.

When the other four walked in together, in a group, Claire knew they'd already heard.

They sat down with her, all wearing grim faces. "So, you're really marrying him?" Jessie asked.

Claire wished they'd be happier for her but she couldn't blame them. Not really. She'd feel the same if she'd heard one of them was leaving the community, and Donovan didn't have the best of reputations. "I am. We're getting married soon and it's a Friday wedding." She gave them the hoped-for date.

"Well, congratulations," Olive said in a rather flat tone.

"Look, I know what you're all thinking, but he's changed. He really has."

Lucy said, "It's just that we're worried about you, and we don't know him."

"I do," Jessie said. "I know enough about him to think you're making a mistake."

The girls gasped at Jessie's words.

"I'm sorry, but one of us has to say what we're all thinking."

Claire wiped a tear from her eye. She'd wanted their support and now none of them were going to be there for her.

Olive, who was sitting next to her, put an arm around her shoulder. "Don't be sad."

"I don't want to end up alone and miserable like Sally."

"I thought that too, but then Elijah appeared even though he was there all along. I'd given up on him. Perhaps there's someone in the community you've overlooked too?" Jessie asked.

Claire shook her head. "It doesn't matter. I love Donovan and I truly believe he's the man for me. Now, I would like it if you'd all come to my wedding, but I understand if none of you can. I know you might not even be able to talk to me at all, since I've left now."

"We'll be there. Well, I will," Olive said.

"I think we'll all be there for you, Claire. I'm sorry I said what I did just now. All of us just want your life to be good and happy."

"Thanks, Jessie. I know."

"And look at how you're dressed," said Amy. "That's going to be hard to get used to."

Claire looked down at her long-sleeved tee shirt and knee-length denim skirt. "I don't even know what to wear as an *Englischer*. Mrs. Billings was kind enough to buy me some clothes, but I don't really like these."

"You'll work it out," Amy said. "You look fine."

"*Jah,* as pretty as always," Lucy said. "I'll support you in anything I can, Claire. You'll always be one of my very best friends."

The girls all murmured the same sentiments and Claire felt a little better. "I'll let you all know when we know for sure when the wedding's going to be. It'll be soon. Donovan's working out the final details. He loves to organize things, which is good because I don't like that kind of thing."

"What do your parents think?" Olive asked.

"They were surprisingly fine about it."

"And Sally?" Amy asked.

Claire giggled. "Her too, even more surprisingly. Now, enough about me. Can this be just a regular girls' get-together? I know the bishop won't like you spending much time together with me now that I've left, so this might be the last time we'll be together like this."

"*Jah,* until Donovan joins us," Jessie added.

"I hope it happens," Amy commented.

Claire nodded and then turned to Lucy. "You look like your thoughts are a million miles away. What's been happening with you?"

Lucy felt sorry for Claire. Not one of them was jumping for joy over her news. "I'm sorry, Claire. I'm happy for you, really. My face might say otherwise, but I'm pleased and I wish you a happy marriage."

A furrow peaked in Lucy Fuller's brow as she then explained to her friends, "I have some things I've been worried about. The problem is the farmland around here is diminishing, and the property prices are rising. The young couples getting married can't afford to buy farmland because the developers are paying so much more to turn the farms into suburban lots."

"*Ach,* Lucy, why do you concern yourself with these things? And why do we need to discuss it here?" Olive clasped her hands on the table in front of her.

Lucy folded her arms and leaned back in her chair at the coffee shop. "All of us should be concerned. What would happen if there were no farmland; what would happen to our way of life?" She looked at each of her friends, Amy, Jessie, Olive and Claire.

Amy moved uncomfortably. "Is it really that bad?"

Lucy fixed her eyes on Amy. "*Jah*, it is. One hundred homes are going up on what used to be Mrs. Hostetler's farm."

"That's only because her *kinner* had left the community before she died and that's why they sold to a developer," Olive said.

Lucy waved a hand in the air, intent on making her point. "*Jah,* and if the developers hadn't offered far and above what a farmer would've paid they would never have sold to them. One, or several, of our fellow Amish would have bought it."

Olive blew out a deep breath. "We can't do anything about it, can we?"

"We can try to stop the developers and encourage owners to keep the farmland." Couldn't her friends see what was happening around them? They had to understand what was going on under their noses; it concerned the whole Amish community and the broader community.

Dan, the coffee shop manager, brought their cakes to them. "The coffees won't be long."

"Thanks, Dan." Lucy smiled up at the man she was fond of. When he left, she went back to what she'd been talking about. "We're the new generation, and it's up to us to save the farmland for our *kinner*." Lucy pursed her lips. She hadn't found a man yet, but Jessie and Elijah were soon to be married and so were Olive and Blake. Claire hoped Donovan would join, but somehow, Lucy didn't think it was likely.

"How's your job with the *Englisch* woman, Lucy?" Olive asked.

Lucy knew Olive was trying to change the subject, but she couldn't force them to be concerned. "Oh! I love it. I'm helping the children with their schoolwork too."

Claire asked, "You do housework for her as well?"

"*Jah,* when the children are at school. And Julie's house is close enough for me to ride my bike."

"Did you hear Joshua Hershberger is back here for his *mudder's* funeral?" Olive looked directly at Lucy.

Lucy gulped. Her family had a long history with Joshua Hershberger. "Is he staying at his old *haus?*"

"*Jah,* I heard he's come back from *rumspringa*, now that his parents have both died, and that he's going to run the farm," Jessie said.

A hush of silence swept over the girls. Lucy said nothing. He hadn't been on *rumspringa,* but she'd let the girls think he had. The girls were quiet because Lucy's sister, Grace, had been set to marry Joshua Hershberger before her sudden death at age eighteen.

"There you go, ladies." Dan placed their coffees on the table.

Once Dan left, Lucy said, "*Mamm* and *Dat* will be upset they missed Mrs. Hershberger's funeral. They would've liked to have seen Joshua too, I'm sure. I hope it's true that he's staying on."

"I guess having him back brings back memories of Grace," Amy said to Lucy.

"I was eleven when she died. I still think of her every day and I can still remember how in love she was with Joshua." Lucy looked up at the ceiling and blinked back tears. "She died three months before she was to marry him." It wasn't only his life that had changed after Grace's death from Swine Flu; Lucy's life had never been the same. Their whole family had suffered.

Olive patted Lucy on the arm. "Elijah told me that's why Joshua left the community; he was distraught. He left the day after her funeral."

Lucy nodded. "And this is the first time he's been back."

"Joshua's *vadder* died some time ago, didn't he?" Jessie asked.

"*Jah,* Joshua would have been fifteen when he died," Lucy said.

Claire frowned. "Joshua left his *mudder* all alone this whole time?"

"*Nee,* she was close to her *bruder* and her *schweschder*-in-law; she wasn't alone. That's where Mrs. Hershberger's body will be for viewing, at their *haus,*" Jessie said.

"He shouldn't have left her alone, that's all I've got to say." Amy wrinkled her nose. "I would never leave my *mudder* alone if I had no siblings."

"You can't hold that against him, Amy. Everyone does what they think's right. My *vadder* says people must make their own way and do what's right in their own eyes," Claire said.

Amy tapped Olive's arm to gain her attention. "You seem to know a lot of what's happening with Joshua Hershberger."

"Elijah and Joshua were friends before he left the community. Joshua came to the *haus* to see him yesterday." Olive picked up her mug of coffee.

Lucy turned to Jessie. "Did you see him? Were you at their home when he visited?" Lucy guessed Jessie might've been there since she was practically engaged to Olive's brother, Elijah.

Jessie nodded. "He's very handsome."

Olive giggled. "He's not as handsome as Blake, though."

Amy dug Olive in the ribs. "You'd have to say that. Anyway, looks are superficial and don't matter."

Olive smiled. "Funny thing is, when you're in love with someone they grow more handsome. When I first saw Blake, I could see he was handsome, but now I think he's the most handsome man in the world."

"It's true; that's what I think about Elijah," Jessie said.

Olive pulled a face at the mention of her older brother being handsome.

"Stop it, the two of you. You're both being boastful." Amy crossed her arms and pursed her lips.

The other four girls laughed at her expression.

Jessie looked at Amy and Lucy. "You two will find someone to marry soon. Months ago, we all had no one, and now, I've got Elijah, Olive's got Blake and Claire is about to marry Donovan."

"I suppose you're right. Anything could happen." Amy turned to Lucy. "Don't you think so, Lucy?"

Lucy shrugged her shoulders. "Maybe. I'm more concerned over if my parents got the message Mrs. Hershberger's funeral is on Friday."

"They probably wouldn't turn around and come straight back. They'd stay for your aunt's wedding, wouldn't they?" Amy asked.

"I guess so. Maybe *Dat* would come back and leave the others there." Lucy hoped someone would return so she wouldn't have to go to the funeral alone. "Anyway, let's talk about something else."

Amy squared her shoulders and looked directly at Lucy. "Okay, Lucy, this question is for you. If Dan joined the community, would you like him?"

Another flurry of giggles went up amongst the girls.

Lucy frowned and whispered, "Sh, he'll hear you." Why weren't they more serious? Okay, so they guessed she liked Dan, but he wasn't Amish, so there was never anything going to happen between the two of them. Claire had given up on finding an Amish man, but she wasn't about to.

Four sets of eyes were on Lucy waiting for her to say something about Dan. Trying to avoid the question, she said, "I want a man who's dependable and Amish or I shall not have one at all. I'm not like you girls; I don't need a man to make my life perfect."

"But you do want *kinner*?" Olive asked.

"I do, but if it's going to happen it will. I will not marry someone I have no respect for just so I can have *kinner.* I simply won't." Lucy realized her voice was high-pitched when the other girls looked at each other with raised eyebrows. She was normally quiet, but this problem about the diminishing farmland had riled her. It also upset her that not one of her friends cared. They would care—eventually, but by then it would be too late.

"*Nee,* you wouldn't marry someone you don't respect, Lucy," Claire said while patting her arm. "No one would like doing that."

Lucy picked up her coffee and took a mouthful. Maybe she should have had a tea rather than strong black coffee; she'd already had two before she left home. It could be that her irritability with the girls was caffeine-related.

The girls chattered on about weddings while Lucy plunged her fork into the pink-iced cupcake in front of her. How would Joshua have changed after all these years? Would he look the same; would he even be the same person after years of living as an *Englischer?* Lucy remembered he was tall and lanky with wavy hair and brown eyes.

Joshua had always been kind to her. Joshua and Grace had taken her with them on many outings. Her favorite memories were a Mud Sale and a night of ice-skating. Lucy closed her eyes and saw Grace and Joshua on the ice together. They had been so in love it was no wonder he fell apart after Grace's death. It was too much for any of them to cope with.

When her cupcake was nearly gone, and she noticed a lull in the conversation, Lucy said, "My *familye* will be in Ohio for three whole weeks."

Concern spread over Jessie's face. "I didn't know

they'd be gone for that long. Come and stay with me, Lucy. You don't want to be all by yourself."

"I can't. I've got to feed the animals and everything." Lucy forced a smile when she realized she sounded somewhat ungrateful.

"Come home with me and I'll bring you back and forth to feed them," Jessie urged.

"*Denke,* that's kind of you, but I'm looking forward to the peace and quiet. I've never been alone before. It could be a nice change for me." The other girls were quiet and Lucy felt different from them. Didn't they care about anything, or were they only concerned about marriage? "Did you know there's a Land Preservation Trust?"

Amy and Jessie shook their heads at her talking about the land again, but Olive said, "I think I've heard of it."

Lucy would make them see there was a real problem and that it was important to deal with it now. "It's been set up to keep development away. The land can never have a shopping center or anything like that put up on it if the current owner files for an easement. The trust issues an easement which is binding on all the future owners of the property."

"Hmm. Does that mean people don't own their land anymore and they have no say? What if they sell it?" Amy asked.

Lucy took a deep breath. They were asking questions; that had to be a good sign. "The easement becomes part of the property deed, which is like the property title. The people still own their land same as before. It's just protected from development so it can forever remain farmland."

"Then it stays farmland for all time and if someone buys it they can't do with it what they want?" Amy frowned.

"*Jah*." Lucy nodded. "Well, I suppose they can do what they want as long as they don't want to develop it."

"That sounds like a *gut* idea then, Lucy," Olive said. At last, they were getting it.

"Why are you so worried now if people can do that?" Amy asked.

"It's been in place since the late eighties. I just wish more people would get involved and not sell off their land for the highest price without considering the consequences."

"You can't force people," Jessie said. "Mark will take over when *Dat* retires, but I don't know if he'd sign the land over, or do the thing you're talking about."

Lucy scratched the back of her neck thinking about Jessie's older *bruder*, Mark, and him taking over his father's land. She explained to her friends the Amish population had doubled in the last twenty years, yet their farming land had diminished. What would happen in another twenty years when their future *kinner* had grown into adults and if the community kept growing as well? If this generation didn't preserve the land now, it might be too late.

"Are you going to the Mud Sale, Lucy?" Jessie asked as if she hadn't heard a word.

Lucy decided it was best to keep quiet on the subject of development for the moment. At least the Mud Sales were a good cause. The money from the auction went to the volunteer firefighters.

"It shouldn't be raining this year like it was at last year's sale," Amy said.

Lucy nodded and stared out the window. Jessie said, "*Mamm* and I made cakes to sell."

The other girls spoke on what their families would offer, but Lucy wasn't listening. She wondered if she might see Joshua at the Mud Sale.

When Grace and Joshua had taken her to a Mud Sale years ago, Joshua's *mudder* sold raspberry jam to raise money, and her *mudder* sold cakes.

Claire left the group not knowing how she felt. In the end, they'd all said they'd support her, but she'd been left out of the conversation completely once she'd shared her news. Maybe it was her fault because she already felt like an outsider and had little to offer Lucy by way of advice.

In her heart, she knew none of the girls believed Donovan would join their community, and maybe he never would. God would not turn His back on her just because she wasn't baptized Amish. She'd thought about getting baptized, but like many of the young people she had delayed it, intending to wait until she found a husband. Without being a full-fledged and baptized member, she couldn't be officially shunned, she reminded herself. Therefore, her parents had the choice whether to associate with her or not. They'd welcome her back for visits, and she was waiting on an answer as to whether they'd attend her wedding.

Events like Amish funerals and weddings were something she'd have to avoid. Claire was sad she couldn't go to Mrs. Hershberger's funeral. Joshua's *mudder* had always been a kind woman.

When Claire was in a taxi heading back to Donovan, she felt much better. Now, with Donovan was where she belonged. She had to put her old life behind her. It felt odd to be the first of her friends to marry since Olive and Blake, and Jessie and Elijah had known each other for longer.

Chapter Fifteen

When Lucy arrived at Mr. and Mrs. Esch's *haus* for the viewing before the funeral, she was well aware she was the sole representative from her *familye*. Olive had invited Lucy to go with her in her *bruder's* buggy. Surely her father would've been there if he'd gotten her message. The late Mr. Hershberger and her father had grown up next door to each other and had been like brothers. Lucy hadn't even received word her family had arrived in Ohio, so there wasn't much chance one of them would suddenly appear at the funeral.

Her heart thumped in anticipation of seeing Joshua, whom she hadn't seen in years. What would she say to him? He'd already had so many losses, and he was only in his late twenties.

At an Amish funeral, it was commonplace to see hundreds of people, and dozens of buggies lined up in the front field in rows. Lucy stepped into the crowded house and at one end of the room she saw the wooden coffin containing the body of Mrs. Hershberger.

Lucy did not want to look into the coffin. Instead, she

stood by the back wall and looked around for Joshua. Then she spotted him. Being the only *Englischer* in the room, he stood out as he talked with the bishop. The rumors about him coming back into the community weren't true, Lucy guessed, going by his clothing.

Jessie was right; Joshua had grown into a handsome man. Lucy's memories of him were fuzzy and were always of him with Grace.

She closed her eyes, the same questions echoing in her mind. *Why do people have to die? Why did Grace die so young?* When she opened her eyes, she saw Joshua walking toward her.

Her feet wanted to run, but she was grown up now and had to control her natural impulses.

What will I say to him?

Joshua was better looking than any Amish man should be. Instead of the bony teenager Lucy remembered, he was bigger, well-built and taller.

He dipped his head when he reached her. "Lucy?"

She giggled. "*Jah*, it's me."

"You're all grown up."

"That's because you've been gone for a long time."

He glanced around. "Where are your folks?"

"*Mamm's schweschder* is getting married in Ohio and the whole *familye* has gone. They left a day before your *mudder* went home to be with *Gott*. I sent a message to them, but I haven't heard back." Lucy licked her lips. "They'll be sad they missed it."

His eyes fell to the floor as if he were disappointed.

"They will be upset to miss the funeral, I know it," Lucy repeated. "They remained close friends with your *mudder.*" Lucy's eyes traveled around the room searching for something to say.

"*Denke,* Lucy, for your kind words." He laughed. "I can't believe how you've grown up."

There was a silent moment. Lucy had run out of things to say. She could not talk about Grace, and she knew Joshua was thinking of her at that very moment.

"If you'll excuse me, I'd better go and speak to some people," he said, drawing his eyes from her.

Lucy nodded and watched him walk away.

Jessie came up beside her and whispered, "What do you think of him, Lucy?"

"He's my dead sister's fiancé," Lucy hissed before she could stop herself. What more could she say? It was a fact. He might be handsome and nice, but he was off limits for more reasons than one. She knew her friends had their minds on getting Amy and her matched up with someone. And, Olive had set a strange pattern with Blake deciding to become Amish. If Olive had chosen someone already within their community, she was sure Claire wouldn't have fallen for Donovan. She and her friends were concerned over how that would turn out. "And he's an *Englischer.* Look at his clothes; he can't be coming back to the community."

"*Jah,* you're right. It seems it's the handsome ones who always leave." Jessie sighed.

Lucy smiled at Jessie's words; she always saw the peculiar side of things.

Joshua sat down in the front row, and then everyone took their seats and waited for Amy's *vadder,* the deacon, who was about to deliver one of the two sermons.

The large living room had been stripped of furniture and it had been replaced with rows of wooden benches, which faced the coffin.

The deacon spoke about how life is a fleeting moment and our real life is with *Gott* in heaven. Twenty-five minutes later, he sat down and the bishop took his place to deliver another sermon. The bishop explained how life was a cycle and everything had a season; there was a time to live and a time to die.

This was different from other funerals. Normally there was the viewing and then the burial, then everyone went back to the family's house for a meal. Were these sermons for a reason? Maybe to encourage Joshua back to the fold?

At every funeral since Grace had died, Lucy's thoughts turned to her. Her only comfort was the knowledge she'd see Grace again someday.

Lucy knew what the bishop said was true in theory, but why was it Grace's time to die when she was so young? Why did Mrs. Hershberger have to die before she saw her son just one more time? Why was *Gott's* timing seldom in line with everyone else's?

Shortly after Grace's death, Lucy had been compelled to ask the bishop if he had answers to her questions about *Gott's* will and *Gott's* timing. The bishop's only answer was that His mind is higher than our minds. There was no way we could fathom *Gott's* reasoning, he had told her.

The bishop closed with a lengthy prayer, and Joshua's mother's coffin was closed. Four men came forward to carry Mrs. Hershberger to the long horse-drawn funeral wagon. Abel Esch, Abraham Miller, Tony Graber and

Jebediah Yoder were the four men chosen to carry the coffin and fill in the grave at the cemetery.

Lucy stood and watched the tall men dressed in black suits easily lift the coffin onto their shoulders. The men held the coffin at each end to guide it through the narrow doorway. Once they were outside, they stood two at each side and heaved the coffin up on their shoulders once again.

After a few moments, everyone filed outside the *haus* and into their buggies to follow the wagon to the graveyard.

Lucy stood outside the house and watched the goings-on. She stepped back and leaned on the side of the house. She had been to many funerals, but this one reminded her of Grace even more because Joshua was there.

"Are you all right, Lucy?" Lucy looked up to see Olive.

"*Jah,* I'm okay." Lucy didn't tell Olive this particular funeral was bringing sad memories.

"Well, come on. We have to leave now if we're to follow the wagon." Olive linked arms with Lucy and walked with her to Elijah's waiting buggy.

Once Lucy was in the buggy, she looked around for Joshua and couldn't see him anywhere.

He must be in one of the front buggies. Surely, he wouldn't have driven his car. Nee, he would not have a car at his mudder*'s funeral.*

She turned and saw a car that must have been his, parked behind Mr. and Mrs. Esch's house.

Elijah's buggy was at the end of the procession and Lucy estimated there would've been more than forty buggies in front of them. When they arrived at the cemetery, Olive and Lucy went on ahead while Elijah secured the horse.

The same four men pulled the coffin out of the wagon and carried it to the freshly dug grave. When everyone had gathered around in a circle, the bishop read out a hymn. When the bishop finished, the coffin was lowered into the ground by ropes. Joshua stepped forward and threw a white lily onto his mother's coffin before the dirt was shoveled in.

Lucy slipped away to visit her sister's grave. It was the custom of her community not to mark the graves with names, but a plan was kept of who was buried and where. Lucy knew exactly the grave where her sister, Grace, lay. Even though years had passed, Lucy was still irritated Grace never got to live out her life.

As she stood at the foot of the grave, she whispered, "I miss you, Grace."

Home life hadn't been the same, ever since she'd gone. Seldom a day went by without Grace's name being mentioned. Lucy knew it wasn't her parents' fault, but everything she did or said was compared with Grace.

Nearly every day Lucy heard how she looked nothing like Grace. Grace had been tall with fair hair, and Lucy's hair was darker and she hadn't grown as tall as her sister. Lucy knew she didn't measure up in her parents' view. She often wondered whether they would rather she'd been the one who died rather than Grace. Why hadn't *Gott* taken her home? Sometimes, she felt guilty she was left alive and Grace was gone.

Murmurings from the crowd behind her told Lucy everyone was making their way back to their buggies. Lucy took a moment to say a few more words to Grace and when she turned around, she came face to face with Joshua. His face drained of color when his eyes fell on Grace's grave.

He stepped forward. "Are you all right, Lucy?"

Lucy turned from him and sniffed, and then looked up at him. "I'm all right. What about you?"

He smiled and nodded. "Death is a part of life, as the bishop says. I've gotten used to it. First my *vadder,* then Grace, now *Mamm.*" He looked down at Grace's plot of dirt and took a deep breath, letting it out as a long sigh.

"I'm sorry about your *mudder.*"

"Denke, Lucy."

Joshua looked over his shoulder at the crowd of people leaving.

"Are you coming, Lucy?" Elijah called out from a distance. Lucy waved to tell him she was coming.

"I'll walk you over." As they ambled to Elijah's buggy, Joshua asked, "Will you be at the Esches' *haus* for the meal?"

"I will."

Joshua said, "*Mamm's* place wasn't in good enough order to have a lot of people over there. I need to get to work and fix it up."

"You'll be staying on then?"

Mrs. Esch interrupted Lucy. "There you are, Joshua. The bishop's looking for you."

He turned to Lucy. "I'll talk to you soon, Lucy."

Lucy hurried to Olive and Elijah, not wanting to keep them waiting.

"Is Joshua okay?" Olive asked when Lucy climbed into their buggy.

"*Jah,* he's good."

On the way to the Esches' house, Lucy's mind wandered to the last days of Grace's life. She'd been sweating and sick with fever for days and was bed-ridden. Then the vomiting began, and she suffered from delirium; things she said had made no sense. The doctor visited every day, and he sent for the ambulance when he saw she was worse. By the time the ambulance arrived, she was already gone.

Lucy had sat in the living room when the paramedics took Grace past her. They had fully covered her body in a white sheet. And just like that, Grace left this world and left Lucy without a sister and her parents without their favorite child.

Joshua had visited Grace every day, but that day he'd been held up. He arrived just as the ambulance pulled away from the house. He walked into the house and from the look on his face he'd guessed what had happened and Lucy's father confirmed it. Three days later, Grace's body was in a pine box in their home for the funeral, just like Mrs. Hershberger's body had been at her brother's house today.

Lucy had not cried until the day of Grace's funeral. Lucy remembered Grace lying there dressed in white, her face expressionless and cold. Grace had always found every reason to laugh and have fun, but the Grace in the coffin seemed like someone else. Lucy had to turn away. Never again did she look at the dead at any of the viewings since then. Lucy learned what heartache was after her big sister had been taken away. Even though Grace was many years older than she, they had been close and losing Grace had left a black gaping hole in her heart.

* * *

When they arrived back at the Esches' *haus,* three tables were spread with food. Most every family had brought food to contribute to the meal. There were raisin pies, cold cuts of sliced meats, varieties of cheeses and breads. The meals after the funerals were kept easy and simple.

Every time Lucy looked over at Joshua, he was speaking with someone different. Joshua caught her looking at him, smiled and nodded. Lucy smiled back then looked away. If she hadn't known he'd been so in love with Grace, she would've thought he was attracted to her. She certainly felt that way about him. Or maybe there was just a bond there because they'd both loved Grace.

When the crowd had thinned, Lucy and Olive went to say goodbye to Joshua.

"I'm sorry my parents couldn't be here, Joshua. They would've wanted to be here and they would've loved to have seen you." Lucy wanted to emphasize the feelings of both her parents and herself.

"I know they would, Lucy. I'll likely see them when they get back."

"So, you're staying on?" Olive asked.

Lucy suppressed a smile when her friend asked the very thing she was anxious to know.

"I reckon I'll stay for a time at least," Joshua said.

Olive and Lucy said their goodbyes and went to find Elijah.

It was late at night and Lucy did not look forward to going back to a dark, empty house. Her mind was numb while she listened to the clip-clop of Elijah's horse heading to her house. "Funerals are always good places to see people you haven't seen in a long time," Elijah said, as he drew into the road leading toward Lucy's house.

"Like Joshua?" Olive asked.

"*Jah,* he's been missed."

"You can let me out here, *denke,* Elijah," Lucy said when they didn't have far to go.

"*Nee,* Lucy, it's too dark. I'll take you to the door."

"Do you want me to come in with you?" Olive asked.

"*Nee*, I've got the lamp near the door. I'll put it on quickly."

"You're sure you won't come back and stay with us, just for tonight?"

"*Denke,* Olive, but I'm determined to enjoy my peace and quiet."

Lucy stepped out of the buggy, glad the day was drawing to a close.

"We'll wait until you get a light on," Elijah called out.

Lucy opened her door and reached for the light. She struck a match and lit the wick then held it up in the doorway to show them she was okay.

After Elijah turned the buggy around and started back up the road, Lucy closed the door and put the main living room light on. Had her parents got word about the death of Mrs. Hershberger? They were very close to her and after Joshua left the community they had made sure his *mudder* had everything she needed. Lucy had often gone with her mother on her visits to Mrs. Hershberger.

She wandered into the kitchen and placed the kettle on the stove for a cup of peppermint tea. Lucy had eaten far too much throughout the day and peppermint tea always soothed her tummy.

Tomorrow was Saturday and her employer, Julie, had let her swap days to attend the funeral, so she had to work tomorrow in place of today.

When the kettle whistled, she took it off the stove and poured the hot water over the muslin pouch filled with peppermint leaves. As it steeped, she watched the steam rise into swirls above the teacup. She hoped to see Joshua again soon. She did find him attractive, but she was sure he still saw her as an eleven-year-old child. Lucy stirred her tea.

Chapter Sixteen

The next day, Lucy was up at six o'clock feeding the animals and doing all the chores before riding her bike to Julie's house. Her *mudder* normally did the morning chores and could take her time to do it, but Lucy had to do everything quickly to make sure it got done As always, Julie's children—Liam and his sister, Tia— ran out to meet her when she arrived. Five-year-old Tia was quiet and liked to color and would sit with crayons and paper all day long if she could. Eight-year-old Liam loved to play in the dirt with his toy trucks.

Julie had planned to go out that day, but the children greeted Lucy with the news their mother was sick. She had come down with a bad cold.

Lucy got the children busy and then crept into Julie's room. "Can I get you anything?"

"No thanks. I was up earlier giving the children breakfast and had something to eat. I felt dizzy and came back to bed. I'm so glad you're here today."

"I'll check back on you in a while."

Julie's eyes flickered and closed. "Thanks."

Just as she was about to close Julie's door, Julie asked, "Oh, Lucy, how was the funeral?"

Lucy poked her head around the doorway. "Much the same as any funeral, I suppose."

"Was the lady's son there?"

"Yes, he was." Lucy noticed her eyes had closed again. "I'll tell you all about it later when you're feeling better." Lucy closed the door.

The children were unusually quiet, so Lucy crept up the hallway and peeped around the kitchen door to see what they were doing. Liam was making himself a piece of toast and Tia was coloring quietly at the table. Lucy stepped into the room. "Liam, are you allowed to make toast on your own?"

Liam looked up from digging a knife into the butter. "Yes, Mom lets me."

Lucy stepped forward and took the knife out of his hands. "Your mother said you've already had breakfast."

He looked up at her with large brown eyes. "I'm hungry again."

"Me too," Tia whined.

"All right, I'll make you both some toast."

"Can I have strawberry jam on mine?" Liam asked.

Tia ran to stand beside Liam. "Mine too?"

Lucy made the children toast and while they ate it, she put on a load of laundry. Lucy kept the children entertained in between washing clothes and other cleaning duties and kept checking back on Julie.

Lucy had been at Julie's house for longer than usual when she looked into Julie's bedroom again. "How are you feeling now?"

"A little better, thanks."

"I can stay longer and give the children dinner."

"Could you? That would be great."

Lucy nodded. "I'll bring you some too. Let me know if you need anything else."

"Thanks, Lucy, I don't know what I'd do without you."

After Lucy gave everyone dinner and put the children to bed, she was ready to go home and it was pitch black outside.

"I'll go now, Julie, unless you want something?"

"No. Thanks, Lucy. I'll pay for a taxi for you to get home. Take money out of the jar in the kitchen."

"I've got my bike here. It's not far and there's rarely any traffic this time of night."

"No, Lucy, it's too late, and it's too dark out."

"Don't concern yourself with me, Julie." Lucy stepped closer to Julie. "Do you want me to stay the night? I could if you want. There's no one at home."

"No, I'm feeling a bit better. I just needed some sleep and having you here made that possible. I'll be better tomorrow, I'm sure of it. Thanks for doing everything."

"You're welcome. Goodnight then, and I'll lock the door behind me so you don't have to get out of bed."

After she checked on the two sleeping children, Lucy closed the front door. She did not like riding her bike at night because she found it hard to see once the streetlights ended and the Amish settlement began. Her father had hooked up a light on the bike for her, but it didn't work very well. She would pull off the road if she saw a car approach.

When she was only five minutes along the darker section of road, she saw the headlights of a car behind her. She moved to the side of the road and was about to get off the road completely except the car speeded up before she had a chance.

She turned to see how close the car was and head-lights blinded her. The car swerved and clipped her bicycle in the rear. Lucy was tipped off her bike and put her hands out in front of her to save her head from hitting the gravel.

As she lay on the side of the road, she heard the offending car screech to a halt. She pushed herself up with her hands and pain shot up her right arm. She heard someone yelling and a fuzzy figure ran toward her.

"Are you all right?" Two large hands lifted her to her feet.

"Ow! My arm and my leg! I think they're broken."

"Is it you, Lucy?"

In the darkness, she stared up into his face. She could barely make out who it was, but she knew the voice. "Joshua?"

"Oh, no, my little Lucy. What have I done?" He held her in his arms. "Are you all right?" he asked again. "Are you hurt anywhere else?"

"*Nee*, I don't think so."

"I'm so sorry. I can't believe I've done this."

She was in too much pain to respond.

He released her and said, "I'll take you to the hospital."

She clung to him because she could put no weight on the one leg. "*Nee,* it'll be okay. I don't like hospitals or doctors."

"You're going to the hospital." He scooped her up into his arms.

The swift motion caused Lucy's heartbeats to vibrate harshly inside her head. "Joshua Hershberger, put me down." She would've yelled, but she was too shaken.

He walked a few paces then placed her on her feet. She yelped in pain when her left leg touched the ground. The only option she had was to lean against him for balance.

"Your leg might be broken."

She looked up into his shadow-covered face. It was all his fault. "Why were you going so fast?"

"I always drive fast around these roads. There's never anyone on them and if there is you can see them for miles." He lowered his voice, "And you don't have any lights or reflectors on your bike."

Lucy hugged her sore arm and tears flowed down her cheeks. She'd been trying to save the battery of the light on the front of her bike. The pain was so intense she was sure her arm was broken. "I never ride at night, that's why. The lady I work for was sick, so I stayed later to help her. I should have caught a taxi."

"I'm sorry, Lucy. Please let me take you to the hospital? Look at you, you can barely stand."

With her face scrunched in pain, she nodded and whimpered, "Okay."

Joshua opened his passenger-side car door. At that point, Lucy wondered what he was doing driving a car. Hadn't he come back to the community? He had said he was going to stay awhile, so was he staying as an *Englischer?* He put her bike in the trunk of his car.

Lucy sat next to Joshua in the hospital waiting room. "I've got your bike. I'll get it back to you. I don't think it's been damaged at all, but I'll check more carefully tomorrow."

"Thank you." She looked down at her clothes to see they were dirty from being scraped along the road. Her good arm had a gravel rash and was red, scraped raw. Joshua was given a form for Lucy to fill out and since she could not write, Joshua filled it in for her. She would sign it the best she could with her left hand.

"I'll put myself down as next-of-kin since your parents are out of town."

Lucy leaned over to see what he wrote. He had written down a phone number. He had a car and a phone and he'd worn *Englisch* clothes the day of his mother's funeral and today he was still in *Englisch* clothes. She didn't need more information than that.

He gave the pen to Lucy, and she signed it with her left hand.

"Ugh, it doesn't even look like my writing."

"I'll guess it'll have to do." Joshua took the form back to the lady behind the desk.

Lucy heard him ask how much longer it would be. There was no one else in the waiting room, so she hoped they wouldn't have long to wait.

He sat back beside her. "They said it shouldn't be too long. I guess we're lucky they're having a slow night."

"*Denke* for driving me here, but you don't have to wait. I can get a taxi back home."

"I'm not going anywhere, Lucy. I've got nowhere else to be." He looked away from her and his eyes fixed in front of him. "No one's at home waiting for me."

She knew he meant Grace wasn't at home waiting.

It was another ten minutes before Lucy's name was

called. She rose to her feet and tried to walk, but the pain was worse. Joshua put his arm around her to ease her foot off the floor. Lucy leaned against him and whimpered.

"Wait there, I'll get you a wheelchair." The nurse came back in a flash with a wheelchair. Joshua went to sit back down and the nurse said, "You can come too."

Joshua followed behind the wheelchair into a curtained-off area.

"The doctor's just finishing up with another patient and he'll be here in a moment." The nurse turned and left them.

When the doctor arrived, he examined both of her arms and her leg, and then they were sent to the other side of the hospital for X-rays.

Two hours later, the doctor came back with the X-ray films. "You have a fracture of the scaphoid bone, which is a fairly common break when you put your hands out to break a fall. You can see where the break is from the X-ray, just down from the thumb." He ran his finger down a white line on the X-ray. "There's no displacement between the bones, which is good."

"I'm glad there's some good news." Joshua scratched his chin. "What about her leg?"

"That's a sprained ankle. You would've got it from a sudden twisting movement that has overstretched the ligaments that surround the ankle, causing them to tear and bleed."

Lucy's hand flew to her mouth as she gasped.

The doctor smiled at her. "It's not as bad as it sounds. It's a common injury, and it's treated with cold packs and rest—lots of rest—and elevation. We'll bandage your leg firmly; you'll need cold packs every two hours for twenty to thirty minutes, and try to keep your foot raised as much as possible. We'll need to put a cast on your arm." The doctor picked up Lucy's good arm to demonstrate what he was about to say. "The cast will start below the elbow and go down to include the thumb and palm. Your thumb and wrist will need to be immobilized."

Lucy nodded.

The doctor left after assuring them they wouldn't have long to wait for someone to put a cast on her arm.

Joshua sprang to his feet. "I should call your parents and let them know where you are. I'll tell them I'll drive you home when we're through here."

Lucy grimaced with pain. "My whole *familye* has gone to Ohio for three weeks. I've already tried to contact them about your *mudder.*"

"*Jah,* you did tell me, but you must have a number for them there." Joshua sat back down. "You'll have to stay with someone."

"*Mamm's* sister doesn't have a phone. I've already left a message with the man she's marrying and I've heard nothing from them." Lucy shook her head. She hated people fussing about her. "And I don't want to stay with anyone; I've been looking forward to the quiet."

"Lucy, you can't walk and you can't look after yourself."

"I can. I'll manage."

Joshua frowned and was silent.

"I need you to do one thing for me," Lucy said.

"*Jah,* anything; what is it?"

"Can you call the lady I work for and tell her I won't

be able to work for a while? Tell her what happened and I'll call her soon." Lucy gave Joshua Julie's name and address hoping he would be able to find her in the directory. Failing that, Lucy did have her number at home somewhere. Joshua was gone for some minutes and returned when she was getting the cast put on her arm. "Did you find Julie's number?"

"Yes, she was in the book. She's going to have her sister stay for a few days. She told you not to worry."

Lucy relaxed. "*Gut,* that's one thing off my mind."

He moved closer to her. "What are the other things, Lucy?"

"Nothing, just how I'm going to manage." She frowned. "Now don't go telling my parents. I want them to have a *gut* time in Ohio. They haven't had a break for the longest time."

Joshua nodded. "Tell me what your job's like."

"I work as a maid for Julie. She's a single parent; she divorced two years ago and her husband moved to another state. She's all alone and has to work full-time and look after her *kinner*."

"Many women do that, and some men. It can't be easy. How long have you worked for her?"

"Only weeks. It was Olive's idea. None of us—well, there are five of us, Amy, Jessie, Olive, Claire and me. Anyway, Olive had the idea we should all become maids because we all had no work and we just stayed at home helping out."

"And you all wanted to do something more?"

"*Jah*, and make a little money, I guess."

"Sounds like a good idea."

"You think so?"

"*Jah*, I do. You're doing a *wunderbaar* thing helping this woman out. And you can contribute to the children's upbringing and when they grow up they'll have good memories of the pretty, young Amish lady who was kind and sweet to them."

Lucy laughed. "You're making me blush. I'm sure."

Joshua laughed. "And did the other girls all find work?"

"*Jah*, they did; all of us did."

"I hear Elijah is going to marry Jessie."

"*Jah*, I think they make a *gut* match. And my friend Olive is getting married to Blake, who came to the community months ago with his little boy. He'll be baptized soon. Then my other friend, Claire, is getting married to an *Englischer*, who said he might join us later—anyway, that's what he told her. She believes it."

"And all of this has happened in the last few weeks?"

"*Jah*, since we all got jobs." Joshua let out a deep breath.

Lucy gave a sideways look. *What's he thinking?* "You've taken my mind off the pain for a while."

He looked at her and smiled. "I'm glad."

The years had given him lines around his mouth from smiling, which only served to make him even more handsome.

Two hours later, Lucy was finally ready to leave the hospital. A hospital orderly wheeled her to the entrance of the hospital. "You have a car?" the orderly asked Joshua.

"Yes. Can I drive it up to the entrance here?"

"You can drive it up here as long as you're just picking up or dropping off a patient."

"Good. Will you wait with her while I get the car?" Joshua asked.

"I can wait by myself, Joshua."

"Yes, I'll wait with her," the orderly finally answered when Joshua kept his gaze fixed on him.

Joshua took the crutches the hospital supplied her with and strode off in the direction of his car. As she sat in the hard wheelchair waiting for Joshua, Lucy wondered about him having a car. She hadn't thought to ask any questions while she was in the hospital; she'd been in too much pain.

Chapter Seventeen

Once they were well away from the hospital, Lucy said, "I'm sorry for taking up all your time tonight, Joshua."

He took his eyes off the road to glance at her. "I can honestly say there was no place I'd rather be tonight than right here with you."

Lucy pressed her lips together to suppress a girlish giggle. She giggled too often around him and if she did it once more he would surely think of her as foolish. "How long do you plan on staying?"

"Don't concern yourself with me; you just rest. Lie back in the seat until I get you home. I still don't know how you're going to look after yourself. Are you hungry?"

"I had dinner with Julie and the children before I left work. There's plenty of food at home anyway."

Joshua took one hand off the steering wheel and rubbed his neck. "I just wish you weren't going to be alone, Lucy."

"I'll be fine." Lucy noticed he had skillfully avoided

answering her question, and she wasn't sure how to bring up the subject again without appearing too interested.

"Are you cold? I can turn the heater up."

"*Nee*, I'm fine."

He stopped the car right at Lucy's front door and sprang out of the car to help her out. Everything was in darkness.

"The front door won't be locked," Lucy said once she was out of the car.

Joshua pushed the front door open. "Where's the light?"

"There'll be a gas lamp to your left on the table."

She heard things being knocked. When she heard a match strike, the room filled with light.

"You won't be able to light a match with one arm," he said.

"*Jah*, I will. I'll hold the box in the fingers of my right hand and strike it with my left hand."

Joshua shook his head. "I'll get you some hot tea and light the fire."

"You should go, Joshua. Some would think it not right, a man and a woman being alone in a *haus*."

"Maybe, except in a case like this I reckon it would be all right." He turned to Lucy and ordered, "You sit down while I do a few things."

Lucy was not very good on her crutches, especially with the modification necessary to protect her fractured hand. It took some time to get to the couch, but when she did she eased herself down, leaned back and wondered how she would sleep.

Once she'd done as she was told, Joshua turned on

the overhead gaslight and took the smaller light into the kitchen with him.

It would be easier to sleep on the couch with a pillow and a quilt rather than climbing the stairs. How would she braid her hair every morning with one arm and no one to help her?

The whistling kettle startled her.

Joshua ducked his head around the corner. "Sugar and milk?"

"Just sugar."

Joshua returned moments later with hot tea and a plate of cookies.

"You're not having any?" she asked.

He shook his head. "I'm not much of a tea drinker."

"Do you mind going upstairs to get me a pillow and a quilt? Just from any room you come to."

While Joshua climbed the stairs, Lucy smiled. They weren't the ideal circumstances, but it sure was nice having a man look after her.

"Here you go; I've got a pillow for your foot and one for your head." He placed the quilt and two pillows beside her then proceeded to light the fire. Once a fire was steadily burning, he sat down. "Can I do anything else before I go?"

Lucy looked at him through the steam of her tea. "*Nee. Denke* for everything you've done."

"I'm so sorry, Lucy. This was my fault. I'll come tomorrow and check on you."

"Could you do one last thing for me?"

"*Jah*, anything."

"Can you let the horse out of the stable and put him out into the field at the back of the barn? I can't keep him in the stable for days, and it doesn't look like I'll be using him soon."

"I've got a flashlight in my car. I'll do it right now then I'll go. See you in the morning."

"Do it in the morning. That'll be okay."

"I'll do it now, so I know it's done."

Lucy nodded, knowing any protests about him doing anything would be ignored. She pushed a pillow behind her head and listened to his footsteps. She heard that he stopped at the door and closed it, then some minutes later she heard his car. She listened until the noise disappeared.

Joshua was years older than she. He'd been an only child, and his parents were older than other parents of children his age. She'd learned from Grace his parents had many stillborn *kinner* and Joshua was the only one who'd survived. That had to make him special in his parents' eyes. It must've been so hard for his mother when he left.

Oftentimes when Grace had come home from being out with Joshua, she would creep into Lucy's bedroom and tell her about their time together. She would speak of moonlit walks, picnics, and Grace told her she would talk for hours to Joshua on all kinds of subjects.

Joshua drove away from Lucy's house, glad he didn't have to stay there another minute. Everything in this town reminded him of Grace and the awful time he'd gone through. He especially didn't need to spend any more time than he had to in Grace's house.

He chewed a knuckle; he could have killed Lucy tonight. She was right; he had been driving way too fast.

The roads were never properly lit once they got further away from the town. He'd been a fool to assume no one would be out.

Now he had to stay here longer than he wanted; at least until Lucy's parents came back from Ohio. He would never forgive himself if anything happened to her. He was responsible, and he had to look after her.

His thoughts turned to his *mudder*. She had died suddenly; during her sleep, he was told. She hadn't even been sick. He should have come back to visit her. He'd made the effort to be here for her funeral; he could've made the effort to come home while she'd been alive. Maybe she died from sadness. She'd been alone and now he was alone. Joshua never considered she'd be gone at sixty-one.

He stopped his car outside his parents' house—the house that would soon be his once all the necessary paperwork was signed. As he trudged up the front steps, he wondered what his life would be like if Grace had lived. They would surely have at least three *kinner* by now. But, life…sometimes life was like a cruel joke. *Gott* had deserted him, he knew that for a fact.

His parents and Grace's parents had been close and they'd wanted nothing more than for Grace and him to marry. Joshua had been swept along in their plans and had asked Grace to marry him. She would have made a fine *fraa*, and the two of them would've been happy.

There was no *gut* reason to rip Grace away from him. He'd done his best to put her out of his mind over the past years, but being back here and especially being inside her home grated against raw nerves.

He had to look after Lucy the best he could. That's

what Grace would've wanted. Grace had had a close relationship with her little *schweschder*, and he had fond memories of outings where they had taken young Lucy with them.

He pushed the door open, lit the lamp on the dining table, lay on the couch and kicked off his shoes. A tiny part of him was glad to be home. He heard scratching at the door and leaped up and opened it. It was Muggins, his mother's beloved cat. "Hello, Muggins. You've come out of hiding to say hello?"

Muggins ignored him and walked straight past him through to the kitchen. Joshua followed him to see him sit by two bowls in the corner. One bowl was full of water, and the other was empty.

"Okay, wait there and I'll find you some food." Joshua wondered exactly how old Muggins was. He was sure the cat must've been five years old when he'd left the community. Opening the cupboard where his *mudder* had always kept the cat food, he found a large container of dry food in the form of pellets. He could smell fish as soon as he uncovered them. "I guess this is your food, Muggins. Glad it's not mine."

Joshua filled up the bowl and watched Muggins eat. He wondered what to do with Muggins once he sold the house. Who would take Muggins? He wasn't a likeable cat; he didn't like to be petted or stroked, and he eyed people with boredom.

Perhaps he should take Muggins with him. He leaned down besides Muggins and stroked his long silver tabby fur. Muggins edged away, so Joshua stopped. What had his mother seen in the fleabag? "Night, Muggins." Muggins ignored him and Joshua headed back to the couch.

Joshua closed his eyes and thought about Lucy. She was an attractive woman, and if she had not been Grace's *schweschder* she might've been a good reason for him to stay and rejoin the community. Since he'd left, he'd never felt he belonged anywhere and had become little more than a drifter, finding work here and there to earn enough for his expenses. Joshua figured Lucy would not consider him a potential suitor anyway, not given his history with Grace.

Lucy was exactly the kind of woman he could see himself with. She had a spark about her and was gentle at the same time. Joshua chuckled out loud. He hadn't even decided what he would do about the farm, his life or going back into the community and yet he was daydreaming of a life with Lucy. His *vadder* had always said he was a dreamer.

His mind drifted to Grace and the feelings he'd had for her. Were they love, or had his feelings of fondness been born out of a sense of duty? He could not remember ever having the same stirrings in his heart when he had been with Grace as the ones when he had looked into Lucy's eyes tonight.

The morning light streaming in through the open living room window gently woke Joshua. He'd had no intention of sleeping the whole night on the couch but had been so tired he had fallen asleep before he found his way to his old bedroom.

His first thoughts were of Lucy. Joshua rubbed his hands through his hair; he would take Lucy breakfast and help her with the chores. He yawned and remembered the early mornings in the Amish community.

Joshua had gotten used to waking at eight rather than five in the morning. Reaching his hands as high as he could above his head, he stretched the length of his body before he left the couch.

Since there was no food in the house, he decided he'd make a quick trip into town to buy himself and Lucy coffee and breakfast. But first, he would wash, shave and change into fresh clothes.

After his shower, he shaved and as he did so, he considered the advantages of cars over buggies. If he stayed in the community he'd have to hitch the buggy whenever he wanted to go anywhere. Hitching buggies was time consuming, and they weren't convenient to park in town even with the designated buggy parking. Things were so much easier in the *Englisch* world when it came to transport.

He had found his *mudder* had stopped using a horse and buggy, which meant he had no animals to look after except for Muggins. Muggins was a moggy of no particular breeding—a farm cat, who thought he was much superior to that. When Joshua was ready to leave the house, he noticed Muggins sitting by his bowls waiting to be fed again.

"How many times a day are you fed, Muggins? I fed you last night, and you've eaten it all."

Muggins looked at him with large green eyes and meowed a deep yowl.

"All right. I'll see what there is." Joshua opened the refrigerator and saw a small container of meat, which had to be Muggins's food. He made a mental note to buy more cat food for him. He was nearly out of the dry kibble as well.

Joshua saw his mother had installed a cat door in the back door. "You're a spoiled cat, Muggins. You can come and go as you please."

Muggins ignored him.

Chapter Eighteen

Lucy woke suddenly to loud knocking on her door, and before she could call out, the door squeaked open.

"Can I come in, Lucy?"

She knew the voice belonged to Joshua. Then she realized she was still in the same clothes as the night before, and had fallen asleep without brushing out and rebraiding her long hair. "Just a minute." She sat up, wound her hair loosely around her head and placed her prayer *kapp* back on her head. "*Jah*, come in."

"You should keep the door locked."

"*Nee*, we never lock the door." Lucy yawned.

"I've got hot bagels and coffee." He walked over to the couch. "You're not awake yet?"

Lucy hunched her shoulders trying to relieve the pain in the back of her neck from sleeping all night on the couch. "Just now."

"Sorry. I thought you'd be awake before now; it's nine o'clock."

"Oh, I have to feed the animals."

"*Nee*, breakfast first." He sat beside her and placed

everything on the low table in front of them. He ripped open the paper around the bagels then took a lid off one of the coffees and handed it to her.

Lucy saw he'd brought breakfast for himself as well.

She took a sip of the black coffee and felt warmth flood through her body. "This is *wunderbaar*, Joshua, but you didn't have to do this." She looked at him and wondered how he could look good for so early in the morning.

"How's your leg?"

"It's not hurting very much." Lucy gave a little laugh. "Not enough to keep me awake." She looked into his eyes and wished she'd had a chance to clean up before he'd arrived. Although, she didn't know how she would bathe or have a shower with the cast on her arm—she'd been told to keep it dry. She'd have to wash herself in a basin. One-handed. "Are you working today, Joshua?"

"Not today." He drank some coffee.

He never had any proper answers for her, which made her more determined to find out his plans. "Have you come back to run the farm, or have you come back and you're thinking about coming back for good?"

He laughed. "That's a lot of questions for so early in the morning."

Lucy did not laugh and kept her eyes fixed on him.

His eyebrows drew together. "I've come back to figure out what to do with the farm; I thought I told you at the funeral. The Smiths don't want to continue with the lease, so I've got to make some decisions. They tell me Abe Troyer might like to take it on. He might even want to buy it."

"You wouldn't sell, would you?"

"I haven't had enough time to know what to do. I'm not giving it too much thought. First of all, I'm going to fix up the *haus*. After I've been here awhile my mind will be clear enough to make decisions."

"Well, I'm glad you've come back."

"You are?" He held her gaze. "I'm glad too."

Lucy looked away from him and gulped. "Everyone's missed you, Joshua. Now that you're back, you can come to some meetings to help save the farmland."

He looked down into his coffee then looked back at her. "And what are these meetings about, specifically?"

"About stopping the developments on our farming land." He was silent, so Lucy continued, "Haven't you heard what's going on around here?"

He shook his head, and his lips twisted up at the corners. "Tell me."

Lucy told him about the farming land diminishing, the prices of farmland rising and the land being turned into suburban housing lots.

"You can't stop progress, Lucy." He took a last mouthful of coffee.

"*Nee*, we have to save the farmland to save our way of life, for one thing. There are many other reasons too." She narrowed her eyes. "You will support the meetings, won't you?"

"Of course I will, if that'll take the frown off your face." He laughed.

Relieved, she relaxed into the couch.

He bit into a bagel. When he finished his mouthful, he said, "Now, I'll feed the animals for you."

"*Nee*, Joshua, I don't want to hold you up all the day long."

"You tell me what needs to be done." He looked at his watch. "I've got a meeting at eleven and then I'll bring you back some lunch. No arguments."

She gave him the instructions on all the animals that needed to be fed. After he had fed the chickens, the pigs, the dog and the horse, Joshua sped back down her driveway toward the road.

Lucy leaned on the windowsill and watched his car disappear. When she could no longer see him, she decided to wash and look her best for when he came back later in the day.

She slowly made her way into the kitchen and soaped up a cloth in warm water ready to wash herself. Lucy hoped Joshua would return to the community.

Was it wrong she was attracted to him? After all, Grace was gone and life goes on, but would he ever forget Grace? He had never married. Was losing Grace the reason?

He hated keeping a secret from Lucy, but he couldn't tell her his meeting at eleven was with a developer who was delivering him an offer on his farm. Joshua still hadn't decided what to do with it, but knowing what it was worth was another link in the chain to make a decision. He also had to decide whether to go back to his *Englisch* life or return to his roots.

When he left the community, he hadn't meant to stay away for so long, but days had turned into weeks, then weeks into months and before long he had been gone for years. The fact he had been gone so long made it much harder to return. His *mudder* would have wanted him to stay on and work the farm and marry a nice Amish girl, but it was his life, and he had to make the decision for himself.

Mr. Keaghan was leaning against his car outside Joshua's house when Joshua pulled up next to him on the the tick of eleven. They shook hands and went inside the house. Joshua directed Mr. Keaghan to the kitchen table, and they both sat. Mr. Keaghan had a large collection of paperwork that he placed between them on the table.

"Mr. Hershberger, I hope you consider our offer a reasonable one."

"Before we talk further, I must tell you what I told your business partner. I haven't decided what to do, but I would like to know what I could get if I do decide to sell."

"Of course, I understand." Mr. Keaghan wrote a number on a piece of paper. He slid it across the table to Joshua.

Joshua picked up the paper and read the dollar-figure silently. His eyebrows raised, causing deep furrows to form in his forehead.

"As you can see, it's a very generous offer."

"Thank you," Joshua said. "I'll give it serious thought." He rubbed his chin remembering Lucy's concerns. "If I sell to you, what will you do to the land?"

"As you know we're a construction company. We'll put houses on it, naturally."

Joshua grimaced. He thought as much, and what Lucy had said was very much in the forefront of his mind.

"Does it matter what'll become of the land? With this amount of money, you'll be set for life. You'll never have to work again."

Joshua's thoughts swirled. He put his elbows on the table and placed his chin on his fists. He couldn't imagine a life of not working. The work ethic had been instilled into him from childhood and was very much a part of who he was. He did not, however, say as much to the man in front of him. "I'll consider it."

The man stood and reached out his hand. Joshua shook his hand and showed him to the door. As Mr. Keaghan's car pulled away from the house, Joshua knew he had to do a lot of thinking.

A movement on the porch drew Joshua's eyes to the left of him. Muggins was sitting on one of the wooden porch chairs licking his paw. Joshua walked up to him and crouched in front of him. "What do you think I should do, Muggins?" Muggins put his paw down and stared into Joshua's face as if he was trying to understand what he'd just said. "It's a lot of money."

Muggins tilted his head and stared at him some more before he went back to licking his paw.

Joshua's memory was jolted to buy Muggins more cat food. "You think about it, Muggins, and tell me tonight what you think I should do."

Joshua stepped inside his house and walked around looking at all the repairs and odd jobs that needed doing. Maybe it was just easier to sell the farm and buy a smaller house somewhere. Yet, this was the home in which he'd grown up. The place held fond memories and had been a happy home before his *vadder* had died. His *vadder* had been a pleasant, even-tempered man who always saw the funny side of things. He was killed in a buggy accident, and afterward his mother retreated into her shell. She rarely went out after that except for

the gatherings every second Sunday. Even though some
of the ladies from the community visited her at least
three times a week, she was never the same. She even
once told him the spark in her life had been snuffed out.

When Grace died, Joshua knew there was no room
in that house for two broken people. It was after Grace's
funeral he made the decision to leave the community.
His friend, Peter, had left the community six months
before, so he stayed with him until he found work. From
there he'd drifted from job to job, from town to town,
trying to find somewhere that felt like home. But nowhere ever did.

The old house was a mess and every room needed
painting. There was damp coming through the ceiling
in the corner of the kitchen, which told him there was
a leak in the roof. *That will be my first priority.* Tiles
were coming off the bathroom floor, and the boards
and the railings on the porch needed replacing. There
wasn't a ton of work to do, but there were a lot of small
fiddly jobs.

Chapter Nineteen

After Joshua bought groceries and cat food, he stopped in at Lucy's *haus* to give her lunch. "I've got fresh bread, ham and cheese."

"You shouldn't have gotten all that, Joshua. I've got meat and cheese here."

He chuckled. "I'll make you some lunch. How are you feeling?"

"It's hard to do anything, but I'm not hurting too badly anywhere."

Joshua walked straight into the kitchen, and Lucy heard him rattling around. He called out, "It's Sunday today—is the gathering on this week or next week?"

"It's on next week. Why?" She was still on the couch.

"I thought you might get some visitors wondering where you were, if it was today."

Would she be able to hobble out to the kitchen to talk to him better? She'd had to manage a trip to the bathroom during the night, and had done okay with the crutches then—there'd been no choice. As she was deciding if she had the ambition to get to the kitchen, he brought two sandwich rolls out on a wooden bread-board.

"That's way too much for me."

He chuckled. "One's for me."

She smiled and took a roll once he'd carefully placed everything on the low coffee table.

"Here," he said, passing her a napkin.

"Denke."

"Lucy, I feel I owe you an explanation for the sudden way I left all those years ago."

She wondered why he was bringing the past up all of a sudden. She swallowed her mouthful of food. *"Nee,* you don't, Joshua. Everyone knows you were upset about Grace."

He placed his roll back down on the wooden board. *"Gott* had deserted me and nothing the bishop said to me at Grace's funeral made sense. He tried to have me look at things in a different way, but all I knew was Grace was gone, and I felt deeply it was my fault."

He took a deep breath. "I was due to get baptized because the wedding was drawing closer; I couldn't make a decision to get baptized until I knew what else there was in life. I wanted to get out and see what was out there. There's a lot of talk about Amish keeping separate, but separate from what? I thought if there were evils in the world I should know. If I have *kinner,* I will need to tell them what they have to be wary of." Joshua rubbed the back of his neck. "Am I making any sense at all?"

"Jah, I guess." Was he saying there were other reasons he left besides Grace? And now that Grace was gone, who would he consider having *kinner* with? He

must have realized his wounds over Grace would heal one day.

He looked down. "I'm sorry, Lucy. I don't remember why I didn't say goodbye to your *familye* or you. All I remember is my head was in a fog."

"It was a hard time for everyone. It was so unexpected, and that was the hardest part. I kept thinking she would get better, but she never got better; she kept getting worse, worse every day."

"Nothing about it makes sense."

"Maybe it's not meant to. Maybe these things just happen for no reason at all."

"Maybe."

Lucy smiled at him. "Every time I get sad about Grace I thank *Gott* I had a chance to know her at all. I can see you're still upset about it. I mean, I am too, but I guess I've had to learn to handle it."

"I know what you mean." Joshua took another bite of his ham-and-cheese sandwich.

When they finished eating, Joshua took the wooden breadboard back to the kitchen. He came back out with the icepack the nurse had sent home with Lucy. "Now, have you been keeping your leg elevated?"

"*Jah*, I've been lying down with it up on a pillow."

"Sit back and put it up on the table." Joshua pulled the coffee table closer to her, and she placed her leg on it.

"*Gut*. Now, let's put this ice on it." He had the icepack wrapped in two dishcloths, and he placed it on top of her leg.

"There's not much ice left, is there?"

"There's enough for a day or two. Mostly you'll

be able to use this one—they usually re-freeze pretty quickly."

Lucy bit her lip. "I don't know why I haven't heard from *Mamm* and *Dat*."

"They'll be okay. They'll be having a *gut* time seeing everyone they haven't seen in a while."

Lucy nodded. "I hope so. Could you get me some water?"

Joshua went to the kitchen and returned with a pitcher of water and a glass. "I should've thought to leave this beside you."

As he poured water into the glass, Lucy watched the muscles move in his strong lean arms.

"Here you go." He handed her the glass.

"Denke."

"What about trying those crutches out?"

"I tried them, and I can't use them very well at all."

"Yes, you can; you just need practice. They'll help you get around."

"You try and use them and see how you go."

Joshua smiled. "You used them in the hospital after the lady showed you what to do."

Lucy shrugged. "It's complicated, and I forgot what she said. I'm getting worse at using them, not better."

"Where are they? I'll see if I can figure out how they work." He frowned at Lucy. "It can't be too complicated."

"By the end of the couch."

Joshua picked them up and placed a crutch under either arm, but since he was much taller than Lucy he had to slump down.

Lucy giggled.

"Don't laugh. You're shorter than me. Now, I'm trying to remember what the nurse said."

"You've got the wrong leg."

He looked down at his legs. "It doesn't matter which leg."

"*Jah*, it does. It's my other leg. It'll hurt if I use the wrong one." Lucy giggled again as he switched legs and put his left leg in the air.

He frowned at her and said, "I'm glad I'm providing you with entertainment."

"See how *gut* you are at using them."

"She said to put both crutches out in front and then…"

Lucy interrupted him. "The nurse said not to look at your feet."

Joshua looked at Lucy. "Oh. Now you remember what she said?"

"*Nee*, just that bit."

"Do I move up to the level of the crutches or slightly past?"

Lucy shrugged her shoulders.

Joshua placed both crutches about a foot in front of him and then hopped his good foot level to them. "Ah, that's it. I'm still standing and haven't fallen on my face yet."

"Keep going, faster," Lucy urged.

Joshua took another few steps, turned around and took a few more toward Lucy, and by then he'd gotten the hang of it. "Easy. Now, you have a go."

"I'm icing my foot. I'll do it soon."

Joshua placed the crutches by the couch near Lucy

and sat down in an armchair. "What can I do for you now?"

"Nothing today, but you could do something for me the day after tomorrow."

"What is it?"

"There's a town meeting on at the local community center. It's about land preservation. Can you come with me?"

"Okay."

"Really?"

"Of course, I'd like to find out more about it."

Lucy frowned. "You would?" She was used to her friends telling her she was worried about nothing. At last, someone was interested.

"When is it scheduled?"

"Seven o'clock on Monday night."

"I'll drive you there."

Lucy smiled, pleased someone she knew was interested in the same things as she was. "Wait; today is Sunday, isn't it?"

"Yes. So, tomorrow is Monday."

"*Ach, jah.* I'm getting my days mixed up."

He gave her a cheeky grin, and shrugged his shoulders.

After twenty minutes had gone by, Joshua mentioned she should try the crutches.

"Okay, but don't laugh at me if I fall. And you'd better be there to catch me if I do."

Joshua moved the table away from the couch. He stood guard as she used her good arm to push herself up from the couch. Once she was on one foot, he handed her the crutches to put under her arms. "Now put the two crutches out in front of you. Then lean your weight on the crutches and move your good foot forward, level with the crutches."

Lucy did what he said and walked a few steps helped by the crutches. She looked up at him and smiled. "I'm doing it."

He clapped his hands. "Yes, quite nicely. Now back to the couch. You don't want to wear yourself out."

"While I'm up, I'll use the bathroom. Then back to the couch."

She did so, walking carefully there and back.

He clapped his hands again at how well she'd done, put his arm around her and lowered her onto the couch. Closing her eyes, she breathed in his warm masculine scent and pretended he was looking after her because he was her boyfriend.

"Leg up."

His order jolted her from her daydream. He wasn't her boyfriend, and he'd just ordered her to put her leg back up on the table he was pushing closer. She obeyed his orders once more, and he placed the cold pack back on her ankle.

"I guess I should make more ice. I'll dump what's there into plastic bags, ready for you to use. It should only take a few hours for the next batch to freeze."

"*Jah*, you could do that. I'll put this thing back in the freezer and use the ice next time around. This is pretty convenient—no melting water to drip."

He walked into the kitchen. "What would you like for dinner?" he called. Lucy could hear him rustling around, putting ice cubes into bags.

"I don't know. Anything that's there and anything

you can cook." She heard the water running and the sounds of him filling ice trays to go into the gas-powered freezer.

"Well?" she asked.

"Pizza. I'll be back with pizza."

Lucy laughed. "You can't cook; is that what you're saying?"

"Guilty."

"I thought *Englisch* men cooked."

"Well, not this one." He fixed his hands lightly on his hips. "Lucy, do you want to come for a drive with me to get out of the *haus* for a bit?"

"*Nee, denke.* I'm a little tired. You can bring my needlework to me."

"*Jah*, I can do that. Where is it?"

"In the top drawer of the bureau in the corner."

He rustled around in the deep drawer and pulled out a large fabric bag. "Is it in here?" he said, holding it up in the air.

"*Jah*, that's the one."

He brought it over to her. "Okay, you've got water, something to do and you've got your crutches. I've got a few things to do and I'll be back later with pizza."

Lucy smiled. "Sounds *gut*."

He patted her on her shoulder. "I will be back before you know it."

His touch sent tingles through Lucy's body. She wondered if he also felt tingles. Lucy reached for the needlework while reminding herself Joshua belonged to Grace.

Chapter Twenty

Joshua drove away from Lucy clenching the steering wheel, upset with himself. Had he stayed any longer, he would have surely kissed her. Why did she have to be Grace's *schweschder?* She was beautiful and intelligent. She worried about serious matters like the future of the land, something he had to admit he'd chosen to ignore.

How he had wanted to draw her into his arms when he'd been helping her up and then back down onto the couch. She muddled his head so much he had momentarily forgotten about his four o'clock meeting with Abe Troyer. He sighed heavily as he drove toward his *haus.* He looked at his watch, relieved to see it was only two; he had time to run errands first.

Once he arrived at the house, he drove the car into the barn and pulled out three bags of food. Muggins was at the door to greet him. "Hello, Muggins. Don't tell me you're being friendly now after all these years?"

Muggins looked up at him and meowed. "Yes, I've got your food."

He turned the front door handle and kicked the door

open with his foot. After he unpacked the food, he filled Muggins's bowl up with dry cat food and filled his water bowl up to the brim. Then Joshua filled the kettle with water and put it onto the stove.

He'd come back to the community for his *mudder's* funeral and had pretty much decided to sell the family home and their acres of land. But now he'd talked to Lucy, and she had told him about the problem with the decreasing land, so how could he sell? How could he be in part responsible for the decreasing of the traditional Amish way of life? He'd get a larger amount of money by far, but it was money he didn't really need. Mr. Keaghan had said he'd never have to work again, but he wanted to work. All he wanted was to have enough to get by and some left over to help others in need. He knew he had gotten those values from his parents and the values were ingrained.

The whistling kettle took his attention. He unscrewed the coffee jar and spooned two spoonfuls into his mug. He never normally had instant coffee, but it appeared there was no stovetop percolator in the kitchen like there had been at one time. Joshua watched the boiling water dissolve the grains, and then he added a dash of milk.

After he had taken a sip, he wondered what he should do. If Lucy were not Grace's sister, he would surely stay and see more of her. But… He had a good construction job waiting for him, and lived in an apartment that suited a single man such as he was. Could he keep his house and farm or should he lease the land and stay on in the community?

He took another mouthful of coffee and thought again about Lucy. She couldn't have had a boyfriend.

At the funeral, she was with Olive and Olive's *bruder*, Elijah. Elijah was a *gut* friend of his and was set to marry Jessie, so he knew Elijah and Lucy weren't dating. Besides, if she did have a boyfriend he would have been around to visit her, today being Sunday, and Lucy would have wanted Joshua to contact him to let him know of the accident. *Nee, she can't have a boyfriend, I'm certain.*

What would Lucy think of him if she knew he had been considering selling to one of the developers she was so concerned about? He figured she would never have to know.

Joshua stood up and ripped open the packet of chocolate cookies that he'd just bought. *What does she think of me?* He sank his teeth into a cookie.

At four o'clock, he heard hoofbeats and then Abe Troyer knocked on his door.

"Come on in, Abe. Can I make a cup of coffee for you?"

"*Nee, denke.* I just had some at home."

The two men sat, and Abe put forward an offer to buy the farm and an offer to lease.

As Joshua knew it would have been, the offer to buy was considerably less than Mr. Keaghan had already offered him. He kept quiet about the other offer because he did not want talk to get back to Lucy.

"What if I want to lease you just the land and not include the house and barn, the same as the Smiths were doing?"

Abe put his head down and worked out some things with the pencil and paper he'd brought with him. "It would be $400 less per month."

Joshua nodded. "Can I have time to think on things?"

"*Jah*, of course, take all the time you need. But it would be good if you could decide before the next planting season," Abe said.

Joshua nodded. He knew Abe grew corn and the optimum time for planting corn was usually around middle to the end of May depending on the frosts. Since it was November, that gave him nearly six months. "I'll make up my mind well before then. I'd reckon I'd only need a few weeks. Either way, I won't be farming the land, but I might stay on in the *haus*."

Abe nodded, and stood up. "I'll leave it to you."

Joshua walked him out. "*Denke* for your offer, Abe."

He leaned against the doorpost and watched Abe drive his buggy away from the *haus*. Now it had become real; he had to make decisions. He scratched his head.

"Pizza. I've promised Lucy pizza." Snatching the car keys off the kitchen table he said, "Don't wait up, Muggins."

It hadn't taken long before Lucy had had enough of doing her needlework with only one good hand, and her dominant hand sore and restricted by the cast, so she placed the project back in her sewing bag and buttoned it. She heard clip-clopping of hooves. It wasn't Joshua because he would have driven his car. Lucy pushed herself to her feet, grabbed the crutches and looked out the window to see Olive, and then sat back down.

When she heard her walking up the front steps, she yelled, "Come in, Olive."

The door opened and Olive looked around the room until her gaze landed upon Lucy. "Lucy, what's wrong?"

She walked closer and saw Lucy's bandaged foot and the cast on her arm.

"I had a little bit of an accident."

Olive gasped. "What happened? Are you badly hurt?"

"I fell off my bike. Joshua Hershberger was there and took me to the hospital. I've got a broken wrist, and a sprained ankle."

Olive's eyes glassed over, and she tugged at the strings on her prayer *kapp*.

"It's nothing to be worried about. I'll be fine. Joshua's been bringing me food and he's coming back soon with pizza."

"Are you sure you're okay? Why didn't you call me? I could've looked after you. Come back home with me."

"*Nee*. Don't worry about me."

Olive sat on the couch next to her. "So… Joshua's been looking after you, has he?"

Lucy giggled. "Stop it."

"I've come to tell you some exciting news."

"Go on." Lucy was glad to have some distraction.

"Claire and Donovan are getting married this Friday. Have you forgotten?"

"When?"

"This Friday, at four o'clock. They're getting married at the B&B Donovan's mother owns. We've all been invited, if you'll remember."

Lucy grimaced. "I said I'd go, but I hadn't heard the date was finalized. I'm glad you came to tell me. Are you going?"

"I'm not sure if Jessie or I will be going. Elijah doesn't want me to go, and I'm sure he'll not want Jessie to go. I know *Mamm* and *Dat* wouldn't like me to go since Claire's marrying an *Englischer*."

Lucy tapped a fingernail on her teeth. "I'll go because I said I would. I'll see if Joshua will take me; he's got a car. My *familye* will still be in Ohio, so they won't know where I'm going. *Denke* for reminding me. I would've forgotten."

"It'll be sad for Claire. I don't think any of her *familye's* going and you'll be her only friend there."

"What about Amy?" Lucy asked.

"I haven't spoken to her yet, but you know what her *vadder* is like."

"Jah." Lucy nodded while thinking of how strict Amy's *vadder*, the community's deacon, was. "It'll probably be just me." Lucy looked at her leg. "Olive, can you tell her I'll be there for certain? Someone should be there for her. If Joshua won't take me, I'll get a taxi."

"I will. How much longer before you get better?"

Lucy shrugged. "I have to go back in two weeks for them to see how I'm getting along."

"When can you work?"

"I'll have to get better at using these crutches. Maybe in a few days I'll be okay to help Julie again."

"Can I do anything for you?"

"Yes! You could braid my hair for me. My brush is in my room."

Olive came back with the brush. Lucy turned her body to the side, and Olive sat behind her and brushed out her long, dark hair.

"So, when are you and Blake getting married?" Lucy asked.

"It'll be sometime next year. Hopefully early next

year, but the bishop said six months after he joins us, at least, I guess March or April. It'll be past the traditional wedding season, but since he's not a traditional Amish man it probably won't matter." Olive smiled. "Are you sure I can't get you anything?"

"*Nee*, I'm fine."

Olive continued to brush Lucy's hair. "I feel bad I came up with the idea of us all being maids. I never would've met Blake, so it's good in that regard, but what about Claire?" Olive shook her head.

"There's also Jessie."

"*Jah*, but Jessie and Elijah would've gotten together eventually. It was just a matter of one or the other making the first move."

"You can't blame yourself, Olive. It was nothing that's your fault. Claire made her own choice. She might've met Donovan anywhere."

"Yeah, but she didn't. It was my stupid idea that forced them together."

"*Nee*. Don't think like that. It was just circumstances, and who knows? It might work out well for her. Donovan could surprise us all. Claire's not a stupid girl, and *Gott* works in mysterious ways."

"You're right." Olive sighed. "*Denke* for saying that." She abruptly changed the subject. "I don't remember much of Joshua."

"We both would've been around eleven when Grace died and he left the community."

Olive said, "He's changed into a man."

"That's what I thought when I saw him. He was so skinny, and now he's quite solid and manly." Lucy caught herself and reminded herself not to sound so excited when she spoke of Joshua. She did not want Olive to know how she felt about him. Even though Olive was one of her closest friends, some things were better left unsaid.

"He might stay on in the community. That's what he told Elijah," Olive said.

Lucy turned her head slightly to the side. "What else did he tell Elijah?"

Olive's gaze turned toward the ceiling. "Just that while he's here, he's going to sort out what he wants to do with the farm and decide if he's coming back here. He said he never meant to be gone for so long. He wanted to see what life outside the community was like."

"Olive Hesh, were you listening in on their conversation?"

"*Nee*, but they were out on the porch, and I was sitting near the window working on my quilt. I wasn't *deliberately* listening." Olive laughed.

"What else did you hear?"

"You like him, don't you?"

Lucy closed her mouth and pressed her lips together. She'd shown far too much interest. "All right, I do." Lucy pulled a face. "Is that weird?"

"*Nee* it's *gut*. He's nice and handsome and he would be perfect for you. I was wondering if you saw it for yourself." Olive sectioned Lucy's hair ready to braid.

"But what about Grace?"

"Grace isn't here anymore and you are."

The girls were silent while Olive finished braiding. "There you go, all done." Olive picked up Lucy's prayer *kapp* and placed it over the freshly braided and pinned hair.

"Denke." Lucy turned to face Olive. "But he really loved Grace. I don't want to be his second choice. Even if he does like me, and I don't even know he does, then is it because I remind him of Grace?" She looked into Olive's deep, blue eyes. "I'd never know, Olive."

"Have you told him how you feel?"

Lucy's eyes widened, and she leaned back. *"Ach, nee!* Certainly not. It's not like that. He's coming here helping me out because he accidently clipped my bike with his car."

"What?" Olive screeched.

"Sh. He's coming back here soon. You see? He's only looking after me because he feels guilty for causing me an injury."

Olive fiddled with the strings of her prayer *kapp.*

"You can't tell anyone I like him," Lucy warned.

"Nee, of course I won't. Well, what are you going to do?"

"I can't do anything." Lucy bit her lip. "Of course, I can't. His mind is totally set on Grace still, I'm sure of it."

"Grace has been gone a long time."

"I know. If only he was someone else, or he hadn't been going to marry Grace." She heaved a sigh.

The two girls looked at each other and raised their eyebrows when they heard a car stop in front of the house.

"That'll be him," Lucy whispered.

"Should I go?" Olive asked.

"*Nee*, stay awhile. It will look funny if you leave right away."

Olive nodded and walked to the door. Lucy heard them greet each other in the doorway.

"Have some pizza with us, Olive?" Joshua asked.

"*Nee, denke. Mamm* likes the *familye* to eat together on a Sunday night."

Joshua put the pizza boxes in the kitchen and came back out to the living room.

Lucy smiled as she watched him sit opposite her. Joshua rubbed his hands together. "How's the patient?"

"I'm getting better. Olive has been keeping me company."

"Can I get you some tea or coffee, Joshua?" Olive asked.

"*Nee*, I just had one at home."

Olive turned to Lucy. "How about you?"

"*Nee.*"

Olive sat back down. "You two go ahead and eat; don't mind me."

Joshua sprang to his feet. "You're sure?"

"*Jah*, of course. Pizza is best fresh and hot."

Once Joshua was out of the room, Olive leaned toward Lucy. "Can I go now? I feel awkward."

Lucy shook her head. "*Nee*, please stay longer." Olive rolled her eyes.

Joshua brought the pizza boxes out with three plates. "Go ahead and have a piece, Olive. One's Italian and the other one is chicken."

"Well, they do smell good. Perhaps I'll have just a small piece."

Joshua passed her a plate then opened the two pizza boxes. "Help yourself."

Olive leaned forward and took a slice of chicken pizza. He put two slices of each pizza on Lucy's plate and passed it to her.

"That's way too much for me."

"*Nee* it's not. Eat it all so you'll grow big and strong." Lucy frowned playfully at him, and Olive giggled.

After Joshua had eaten a couple pieces, he said, "It's nearly dark, what do I need to do for the animals?"

"Check on the food for the chickens to see they've still got enough. Also, check their water please and the pigs' water. Bessy likes to make a mess of the water so it might need to be replaced. Then feed them the same amount of food as this morning, not too much, or they will make a mess and they'll spread it everywhere. Give the horse some hay too, please, and make sure he has clean water."

"Will do. That it?"

"*Jah.*"

Joshua excused himself and went outside.

Olive whispered, "I'll wait until he comes back then I'll go."

"*Nee*, stay."

"I'm in the way. I can tell he likes you," Olive whispered.

"Why do you say that?"

"Oh, just the way he talks to you…and how he looks at you."

Lucy took a mouthful of pizza and thought while she chewed. Could Olive be right? Olive did not know Joshua very well; Joshua was her *bruder's* friend and not hers, and even Elijah hadn't been in contact with Joshua for years.

When they heard Joshua coming back, Olive leaned toward Lucy and whispered, "Don't forget about Claire's wedding."

"I won't forget," Lucy whispered back.

Olive turned to face Joshua as he came through the front door. "I'll go now. *Denke* for the pizza."

"You're welcome," he said.

Chapter Twenty-One

"**I**'ve got a favor to ask you, Joshua."

"Jah?"

"Would you go to a wedding with me on Friday?"

"A town meeting tomorrow night and a wedding on Friday? Miss Fuller, you're taking up a lot of my time."

Lucy smiled. "It's one of my friends, Claire, getting married to the *Englischer* I told you about. I don't think anyone else in the community is going. It'll only be me—and you if you'll take me."

"Jah, I'll take you."

"Have you been to an *Englisch* wedding before?"

"Two of my friends have gotten married, and I went to their weddings."

Lucy immediately looked away from him. She shouldn't have mentioned weddings, which would only make him think of Grace.

"What's the matter? You've suddenly gone quiet and you look pale."

"Just thinking of Grace." There, she'd said what they

were both thinking. Things were always better when they were out in the open.

"We both miss people who aren't here anymore, and one day we won't be here anymore. And there's not a lot either you or I can do about it." He wagged his finger at her.

"I know it." She bit on a fingernail. Yes, she knew it, but sometimes knowing it didn't help.

"We have to make the most of the life we've been given, Lucy. Put the past behind us and keep moving ahead."

Lucy nodded.

The next night, Joshua sat beside Lucy at the community center and heard how the developers were buying up land in local farming communities, and building shopping centers, suburban clusters and industrial complexes. All of these changes were impacting the pastoral life of the Amish and other Plain Sect farmers. Even traditional *Englisch* farmers whose land had been passed down through their families. The lifestyle these farmers had passed from generation to generation was slipping away.

Some of the most fertile farming land was now intersected with homes and industry. The farms were getting smaller, forcing many of the farmers to leave the area. Some of the industries were noisy or smelly, negatively impacting neighboring farms too. And they created heavier traffic, a hazard to horse-and-buggy travelers. A college professor showed projections of what the area would probably be like in ten, and then twenty, and then thirty years. The farmland was going to be depleted. Even Lucy, who was well-informed, was shocked.

Joshua knew he had some big decisions to make.

He had the realization of what would happen to his farm, and how it and the area around it would be ruined if he sold to the wrong people. Joshua also had to face the problem that he was falling in love.

All the things that were said at the community center played over in Joshua's mind. His land was a considerable acreage and the developers could divide it into many lots, which meant a sizeable amount of money for him. But that would take prime farmland away from the Amish farmers.

As Lucy kept saying, what would things be like twenty, thirty years from now if farms were continually sold to developers for suburban lots? The Amish would have to divide into smaller groups and more would be forced into occupations other than farming. He could already see the impact just the ten previous years had made on the community. When he'd been a child, most of the Amish people were farmers and they lived mostly off the land. Now, many of the Amish folk had diversified into other businesses, many of them catering to the tourist trade to sell handmade furniture, Amish style food, quilts and handcrafted items.

He could not let Lucy know he'd already had an offer on his land from one of the developers.

Did he care about the future of their farmland? Or would he take Mr. Keaghan's lucrative offer—or one from another of the developers—and continue his life away from the Amish and the memories that caused him pain?

As they walked to his car after the meeting, Joshua said, "Come and take a look at the house, Lucy. I need a woman's opinion."

"I've seen your *haus*, Joshua."

"When was the last time you saw it?"

"It would probably be some months back that *Mamm* and I visited your *mudder*."

"I'll come and get you in the morning. That is, if you don't have any other plans?"

She had nothing to do and was limited in what she could do with an arm and a leg out of action. "*Nee*, I don't, but could we stop by Julie's *haus?* I want to see when she wants me back."

"Do you think it's a good idea? The doctor said to rest. I think you should have a good week off at least."

"I'd just like to visit and see if she and the children are okay. Maybe we could go early before they start school.*"*

"I'll pick you up at eight?"

"Perfect."

When Joshua took Lucy home, she stayed by the door and watched his bright headlights as they traveled back up the darkness of the driveway. She lit a lamp and made her way into the dark kitchen where she flipped the switch of the gas lamp. She pulled out a chair and lowered herself into it. What was she going to do? She was falling in love with Joshua. What if he left the community? He had said on more than one occasion he hadn't made up his mind.

Lucy made her way up the stairs, her first time with her crutches, slipped into bed with a deep sigh, and it wasn't long before she was asleep.

* * *

Joshua was there very early the next morning to feed the animals. He had said he'd fetch her at eight, but he was already there at seven. Lucy heard his car stop outside the house. She stepped out of her cotton nightdress and pulled her dark green dress over her head, followed by her over-apron. Keeping her sore hand very still she managed to braid her hair and place her prayer *kapp* on her head. She had no hope of tying the strings, however, so she left them hanging.

She was too scared to go down the steps with her crutches, so she slid the crutches down and then scooted down on her bottom, one step at a time. Once she reached the bottom step, she collected her crutches and pulled herself to her feet. Just as she did so, Joshua opened the door.

"Ah, you're awake. I was coming in to fix you some breakfast."

"I was just on my way to do the same. There'll be some eggs to collect."

"*Gut*, I'll make us omelets."

Lucy giggled and was glad he hadn't come inside a few seconds earlier to see her sitting on the steps.

After a breakfast of omelet and toast, Lucy visited Julie before the children were to be at school. The children heard the car and came running out of the house to see who it was. Lucy's bandaged foot and the cast on her arm fascinated Liam and Tia.

Julie walked over to them. "Lucy, are you feeling all right?"

"I came to see how you were. I'm fine and I should

be back to work on Monday, but I might be a bit slow." She looked down at her leg.

Julie looked at Joshua, who had just stepped out of the car.

"Julie, this is my friend Joshua. He's the one who called you."

Julie and Joshua said hello to each other. "Can you come inside?" Julie asked.

"No, we won't hold you up. I just wanted to see if you were okay and ask if you want me to start back Monday."

"Yes, please. The sooner the better; as long as you're up to it."

Once Joshua and Lucy were back in the car, Joshua said, "They are two cute kids."

"They are. I've missed them and I've missed Simon and Michael. You remember Simon and Michael?" Lucy spoke of her two younger *bruders*, who were with her parents in Ohio.

Joshua chuckled. "Simon was a baby and Michael was only starting to walk."

"Shows how long you've been gone. They're ten and nine now."

"I have been gone a long time."

After Joshua had shown her around his house, they sat on the porch with coffee and cookies.

"Did you make these cookies yourself?"

"Very funny. You know I didn't."

Lucy chuckled. "They look good." She sank her teeth into a double chocolate cookie. "Mmmm, they are pretty good."

Joshua looked out across his farm. "I always wondered whether I was adopted."

"Why?" Lucy frowned.

"*Mamm* and *Dat* tried to have *kinner* before and after me. They had many stillborn *bopplis*."

"*Jah,* I heard that."

"They insisted I wasn't adopted. They said I was the blessed one, the one who *Gott* wanted to stay with them. Then I left *Mamm* alone. Can you imagine how she felt?"

Lucy took her eyes off him and looked out to the fields. "She would have understood. She was a smart woman. Everyone knew why you left."

"I could've come back; I could've visited, but I didn't."

"You can't change the past, Joshua. So there is no use being sad about something you can't change."

"I know, I know it, but it doesn't change things. I don't feel any better for knowing that."

At that moment, Lucy knew she could not compete with the past. There was no way Joshua could be happy with another woman. Neither did she want to live the rest of her life in the shadow of her sister. It was best she not think of him romantically. "What are you going to do with the land? Are you going to stay and work the farm?"

"I've never been a farmer. I didn't grow up farming like a lot of other children. My parents were older than the parents of other children my age, and from when I was young my parents leased the farm. We kept a small plot of land surrounding the house for horses, chickens and for the vegetables, of course."

"You can learn."

"I don't have the desire. I think I'll lease it out. I'll stick with construction; it's what I'm good at."

"You're not going to leave the community, are you?"

He shook his head. "I haven't decided."

Chapter Twenty-Two

"The wedding will be out in the garden as long as the weather stays nice," Lucy said when Joshua stopped the car outside the B&B for Claire and Donovan's wedding.

Joshua said, "You lead the way."

Lucy walked behind the building into the grounds. It was to be a small, low-key wedding with few guests. Lucy and Joshua were offered champagne or orange juice from a silver tray held by a waiter dressed in a white suit.

"Can I leave you here, Joshua? I want to find Claire."

Joshua nodded. "You go ahead. I'm sure she'll be pleased to see you."

Lucy walked into the building and asked the receptionist where Claire was. Lucy was given her room number and then walked down the long hallway and knocked on her door. "Claire?"

Claire opened the door, and delight spread across her face. "Lucy!"

The girls hugged each other.

"I'm so pleased you're here. The other girls couldn't

come." Claire looked down at Lucy's crutches, the cast on her hand and her bandaged foot. "*Ach*, what have you done?"

"Long story involving falling off my bike. Anyway, I've got a broken wrist, and a sprained ankle." Lucy looked at Claire's dress. "Your dress is so pretty."

Claire smoothed her hands down her sleek high-necked dress. "It's satin and lace." Claire spun around. "I love how it only just touches the ground. It's *Englisch*, but still modest."

"It's beautiful." Lucy had heard none of Claire's *familye* would attend the wedding. She desperately wanted to ask if they had changed their minds but dared not in case they hadn't. "I'm so happy for you, Claire. You look as though you are the happiest woman ever."

Claire smiled. "I'm happy to have found Donovan. I didn't like him when I first met him. That first impression I had of him was totally opposite to the person he truly is. He did tell me he had changed." Claire glanced at the digital clock radio. "Fifteen more minutes, and I'll be Mrs. Donovan Billings."

"That's exciting." *I should tell her now before she sees him.*

"I'm here with Joshua Hershberger."

"That was nice of him to bring you. I was sorry I couldn't go to Mrs. Hershberger's funeral."

Lucy nodded. "Joshua was kind enough to drive me here. He's been doing things for me since I hurt my leg because all my *familye* are at Aunty Becca's wedding in Ohio."

Claire sat on the bed. "I miss the news and knowing what's going on in the community."

Lucy sat next to her. "Do you think Donovan might join with us like Blake has?"

"I think he might, but it's going to take some time. Even if he doesn't, he said we'd never move far from here. We both like it here."

"That's *gut*. All the girls miss you. It's not the same without you."

"I know, but I don't want to get anyone into trouble because you're not supposed to be too close to *Englischers*." Claire smiled and looked down. "That's why the other girls couldn't come today."

"I'm here."

"*Denke*, Lucy."

There was a sharp knock on the door before it opened abruptly. A well-groomed lady poked her head around the door. "Are you ready, Claire?"

"Almost, Mrs. Billings."

The woman looked Claire up and down, then left without even acknowledging Lucy's presence.

Lucy looked at Claire. "Who was that?"

Claire whispered, "My *mudder*-in-law to be."

"You call her Mrs. Billings?"

"*Jah*. She hasn't said to call her anything else."

Lucy grimaced, and then quickly smiled when she saw the worried look on Claire's face.

"She approves of the wedding, doesn't she?" Lucy asked.

"I guess so. She does want grandchildren, and she has been nice to me."

"As long as you and Donovan are happy, that is all that matters."

"Lucy, do you think I'm rushing into things?"

Lucy frowned. It was a terrible time to ask her and how would she know about things such as this? "Do you love him?"

"I do, *jah*, I do."

"And he loves you, and he even said he might join the community, didn't he?"

Claire nodded. "I just think I'd feel better if my *familye* were here."

"Not everything in life happens as we want it to, Claire. We have to hold on to the good and not think too much about the bad." Lucy'd had to learn that lesson the hard way.

Claire rose to her feet. "I didn't plan to have an attendant or a bridesmaid, but will you stand next to me when I'm joined in marriage?"

"Of course I will."

"Well, we had better make a start." Claire rushed to the window and looked out. "There's hardly anyone here. Just close relatives of Donovan's and a couple of Donovan's friends. That's Joshua in the white shirt?"

Lucy stood beside Claire and peered out into the gardens behind the safety of glass and a sheer lace curtain. "*Jah*, that's Joshua."

"He's all grown up. I remember him as skinny."

"*Jah*, he was skinny when he was younger. Now, let's forget about him and get you married." *Yes, let's get you out of this room before you say Joshua would be a good match for me.*

As Claire came to the back of the garden, Mrs. Billings gave the signal for the three musicians to announce the bride's arrival. Lucy walked to the front first, and when she turned around everyone watched Claire as she walked up an aisle made between two groups of fancy white chairs.

The guests sat, and the music ceased when Claire reached Donovan. A male celebrant stepped forward and said a few words. After Donovan and Claire said their vows to each other, they were pronounced husband and wife. Everyone clapped as Donovan and Claire kissed and then the music started up again.

Lucy looked around for Joshua. He caught her attention by raising his hand. From his pleasant expression, he hadn't minded too much that she had practically ignored him the whole time since they'd arrived.

"I'm sorry, Joshua. I got talking to Claire, and she asked me to stand with her. I didn't mean to leave you alone."

"I'm all right. I'm glad to be here with you to see one of your friends get married. There's so much unhappiness in the world; I like to be amongst happy people."

Lucy hoped he wasn't making himself sad again by thinking about Grace.

"Looks like you're getting the hang of those crutches."

"I'm becoming an expert on them. I can go quite fast sometimes."

The celebrations went into the night, and when Joshua and Lucy got in the car to go home, it was well past midnight.

Lucy looked at her house as they approached it from a distance. "I thought I saw a light in the window of the *haus*, and now it's gone."

"Could've been a reflection of the headlights."

Lucy squinted as she looked closely at the house, and there was definitely no light there.

Joshua stopped the car in front of the house and sprang out of the car. "Here, I'll take your crutches." He leaned into the car and took hold of the crutches, propped them on the car and helped her out.

"*Denke*." Lucy noticed his arm lingered around her for longer than needed. Her gaze went from his hand on her shoulder straight into his eyes.

Their eyes locked, and in the moment, she knew he had the same feelings for her as she had for him. A swirling trail of chilling air engulfed them, causing Lucy's body to shiver.

"You're cold." He drew her into his arms.

She closed her eyes and melted into his hard chest, protected by his love.

A sudden noise from the house caused them to jump apart. Their eyes flew to the front door to see the looming figure of Lucy's father in the doorway.

"*Dat*, what are you doing here?"

"Perhaps saving you from doing something foolish."

"Mr. Fuller, I can explain." Joshua stepped toward him, and Lucy took hold of her crutches.

Mr. Fuller looked down at his daughter's foot. "What's happened to you?"

"I fell off my bike."

"Go to your room, Lucy," Mr. Fuller said.

Lucy looked up at Joshua and then walked past her father and into the house. She had never seen her *vadder* not happy to see Joshua. She climbed the stairs slowly, and once she was in her room, she looked down at the two men through her window. She opened the window a crack to listen, hoping she could hear what they said.

"Joshua, I'll have to ask you to keep away from Lucy."

"I don't know if I can do that."

Lucy saw her father looking at Joshua's car. "Are you coming back to join us?"

"I'm not sure what I'm doing. I need some time to sort a few things out."

"What are your intentions toward Lucy?"

"I've fallen in love with her."

Lucy gasped at hearing him confess such a thing to her father.

"Are you going to change your mind about Lucy the same way you changed your mind about Grace?"

What?

Lucy nearly spluttered, and covered her mouth with her hand just in time. He'd changed his mind about her sister?

She listened hard as her father continued, "Her *mudder* thought that was what brought her sickness on, and that was what killed her."

Lucy put her hand to her heart as it thumped harder than ever. They were blaming him for Grace's death.

Joshua's hand flew to his head. "It wasn't like that with Grace. It's what both families wanted, and we both just went along with it. I'm sure Grace felt the same."

Her father shook his head and looked down at the ground. Lucy knew her father would think a man should not go back on his word no matter what the circumstances. He was disappointed in Joshua for breaking Grace's heart.

It all made sense. Joshua was a man of indecision. He couldn't decide about the farm or coming back to the community, and he had changed his mind about marrying Grace all those years ago. Lucy chewed on her lip. Joshua had told her father he was in love with her.

She looked down at the two of them. Their voices were quieter now and she couldn't hear any more. She watched Joshua walk to his car; the headlights beamed. He turned his car around and drove to the road. Lucy watched until the car disappeared. Lucy wondered if her parents disliked Joshua so much they had ignored her message about his mother's funeral.

The front door shut firmly and her father's footsteps headed toward the stairs. "I'll be taking you to work and back from now on, Grace, I mean, Lucy."

Lucy rolled her eyes. *"Denke, Dat,"* Lucy called out. Her parents often called her Grace, and she rarely corrected them. Sometimes, it annoyed her, but she was used to it.

Lucy slipped between the warm covers of her bed, and the conversation between Joshua and her *vadder* replayed in her mind. Why hadn't Joshua been in love with Grace? Everyone loved Grace. Her father was not happy about the idea of Joshua and her together, and it was clear he never would be.

Her stomach churned; she had wanted to kiss Joshua and might have if her *vadder* hadn't been home. Now things had become impossible between the two of them. She could never marry a man without her *vadder's* consent. She wasn't as brave as Claire, and now Joshua had as good as said he hadn't been in love with Grace; he'd never have her parents' approval.

How would she put him out of her mind? It was something she simply had to do. She couldn't put her trust in a man who didn't know his own mind. Grace must've been devastated to find out he didn't love her. From what her *vadder* had said Joshua had called off the wedding. No one had ever told Lucy the wedding had been called off. Joshua must've fled the community through shame and guilt rather than heartbreak.

Lucy put her hand to her head. Her stomach churned, and she knew she had a migraine coming on. She needed to wrap ice in a cloth and put it on her forehead, but she couldn't go downstairs and face her *vadder,* not when he was in this mood.

Still unable to sleep because of the headache, Lucy clunked downstairs with her crutches after she heard her father walk up the stairs and close his bedroom door. After drinking a large glass of water, she unfolded a clean dishrag and placed cubes of ice in it then made her way back up to her bedroom.

The ice eased her sore head once she was lying back in bed, but her body was full of annoying tension gripping her shoulders like a vice. What would she say to her father tomorrow about Joshua? She sent up a silent prayer. She didn't want her parents to be upset with her, and she didn't want them to feel anger toward Joshua.

Joshua drove away from Lucy's *haus* upset at having had unpleasant words with her father. Mr. Fuller had always been like an *onkel* to him. He would never be able to be with Lucy, and without her there was no reason to stay. How could he stay here with Lucy's parents blaming him for Grace's death? If he married Lucy, it would rub salt in their wounds. Besides, Lucy's father had asked him to stay away from her. Everyone would be better off if he left.

Once back at his house, Joshua opened the door and walked to the center of the darkened room to flick on the overhead gaslight. A meow from Muggins came from the direction of the back door. Knowing he'd filled his food bowl twice already, Joshua went to see why Muggins was meowing.

"Hello there, boy. I hope your day was better than mine." Muggins had enough food and water in his bowls, so Joshua walked back into the living room and threw himself heavily onto the couch. "What a mess I've made of things. I should never have told Grace I didn't want to marry her." He sighed. "Now, I've got some decisions to make, decisions that can't wait."

Chapter Twenty-Three

The next morning, Lucy was pleased her headache had gone. Now, she had to go downstairs and face her *vadder*. The sun streamed through her window, which meant she'd slept longer than normal. Her *vadder* would think her lazy for not feeding the animals and doing her chores at the crack of dawn. Even though she was injured, that was no excuse.

Getting washed and dressed was not an easy task when she only had one arm that worked properly; everything took twice the time.

Lucy found her *vadder* in the kitchen. "Morning, *Dat*." She noticed he was making his breakfast. "I would have made that for you."

"You were asleep. *A person who is slothful in his work is a* bruder *to him that is a great waster.*"

"*Jah, Dat.* I'm sorry." Her father often quoted Scripture at her when she did something that made him unhappy. "I'll have something to eat and then feed the animals."

"You can clean my dishes too."

"Okay. Is everyone staying longer in Ohio?"

"I came back when I got word of Ilene Hershberger's death. Seems I'm too late for the funeral, but I came as soon as I could."

Lucy nodded. Normally she would've said Joshua would've appreciated it, but it was best not to mention Joshua this morning.

Her father walked out of the kitchen leaving her alone with the toast she was making. When she heard the front door shut, she looked out the kitchen window to see him heading to the stable. He had surely gone to check his horse she'd had Joshua put out into the field. She knew she had done the right thing for the horse since he hadn't been worked for days. The horse could not stay in a stable for days when he was not being regularly exercised.

Lucy sat down and ate her toast, glad her father hadn't mentioned Joshua.

When he came back inside, she asked him, "*Dat*, could you drive me into town to meet the girls?"

"It's the girls you're meeting? You're not sneaking away to see Joshua?"

Lucy was upset with what her *vadder* said. He wouldn't have said that to Grace or anything of the kind. Lucy had never done anything to show she was untrustworthy. "*Nee*. I wouldn't do that. I meet the girls nearly every Saturday—well, often on Saturdays. *Mamm* knows that."

"What time do you want to be there?"

"Three o'clock and one of the girls will bring me home."

"Very well."

* * *

The whole day had nearly passed with Joshua's name only being mentioned once until they were on the way into town.

"Joshua came back to bury his *mudder* then?"

"Jah, Dat." She looked over to see if she could determine which way the conversation would head.

"What were you doing with him?"

"He was helping me since I hurt myself and he was bringing me home from Claire's wedding. I told you Claire was going to marry the *Englischer.*"

"I thought you wouldn't have gone to the wedding. No *gut* will come of mixing with the *Englischers.* Joshua isn't one of us anymore, so you'd do best to stay away from him."

Lucy clamped her lips together and looked out the window at the fields. Everything within her wanted to see him again and be held in his strong arms. Had Grace ruined her chance at love? Grace should have known Joshua did not love her. And if the two families had not expected Grace and Joshua to marry, Grace might be alive right now, and Joshua might be free to marry her.

Why weren't things simple? She was tired of living in Grace's shadow. Even though Grace had died years ago she was still affecting every part of Lucy's life.

Her father stopped the buggy around the corner from the coffee shop.

"Denke, Dat. I'll see you later. I'll be home in time to cook the dinner for you."

"Bye, Grace."

Lucy was nearly out of the buggy with her crutches on the ground. She gained her balance, turned to her *vadder* and said, "*Nee, Dat.* I'm Lucy; I'm not Grace. I never will be Grace, and I'm sick and tired of Grace ruining my life. I'm alive, and Grace is dead." She instantly wished she could have taken back the words that spilled out of her mouth. Up until now, Lucy had never raised her voice to either of her parents.

They stared at each other for a moment, each as shocked as the other, before Lucy looked down, moved her crutches into position and walked away. She could not apologize for the words because they were true. The words should have been said a long time ago.

Lucy was the first of the circle of friends to arrive, and she sat at the usual table, which Dan had placed a "reserved" sign on. Dan came toward her as soon as she sat down.

"Lucy, what happened to you?"

"Bike accident, I'm afraid." She pointed to the reserved sign. "I hope this is for us?"

"It is. Do you want to wait for the other girls or do you want something now?"

Lucy smiled at him. "I'll wait."

Ten minutes later, the other three girls sat listening while Lucy told them all about Claire's wedding. All the while she felt bad for having spoken so harshly to her father.

"Did you know Joshua's leaving?" Olive asked Lucy.

"When did you hear that?"

"Elijah went to see him this morning, and he was getting the farm ready to sell. Joshua's going to leave as soon as it's sold. He said he's got an offer from one of the developers."

Lucy gasped. "He wouldn't."

Olive shrugged her shoulders. "I know you spent some time with him; did you tell him about what you're worried about with the development in the area and everything?"

"*Jah*, he even went to one of the area meetings with me on Monday."

The girls all looked at Lucy.

"I have to go." Lucy pulled her crutches under her arms. Olive sprang to her feet. "Where are you going? I'll take you."

"*Nee*, I'll go alone." She had to see Joshua and stop him from selling his farm.

Fifteen minutes later, the taxi stopped at Joshua's farm. She couldn't see his car anywhere. She paid the driver and walked toward the house.

After knocking on the door loudly for several minutes, she could only assume he wasn't home. Had she missed him? Had he signed contracts with the developers and then left town? She heard a meow and looked down by her feet. It was Muggins, Mrs. Hershberger's cat. "*Wie gehts*, Muggins? I guess he wouldn't have left you here alone. And if he has, you're coming home with me."

Lucy walked a few steps and lowered herself into one of the porch chairs, and the cat strolled toward her and sat at her feet.

Hearing a car, she closed her eyes and hoped it was Joshua. She opened her eyes to see it was. Joshua's dark blue car stopped in front of her.

"Lucy." He slammed his car door and walked to her. She stayed seated.

"Does your *vadder* know you're here?"

"Joshua, is it true you're only here to sell your farm?"

"I told you I came here not knowing what I was doing. I had hoped that time here would help me to figure things out."

"I heard you're selling your land to one of the developers, Keaghan or Ryan."

"I worked for Mr. Keaghan once. I was considering it; *jah*, it's true. But, now I've taken into consideration everything you're concerned about."

"It's not just me who's concerned, it's thousands of people."

"I've already made application for an easement, so the land of my *familye* will never be sold or used for anything other than farming."

Relief covered her like a warm blanket. "You have?"

He rubbed his chin. "Did you come here to stop me leaving?"

"*Nee*, I was having coffee with my friends when Olive said you were leaving and selling your farm."

He kneeled down in front of her. "You didn't want me to go?"

She looked away. "I didn't want you to sell the farm to a developer."

He picked up her hand and held it in his. "I had words with your father last night. He's not happy about the idea of the two of us. I know I haven't said any of this to you, but I said something about how I feel about you to him."

"What did you say?" She had heard most of it except for the low-pitched words they had spoken to each other at the end.

He smiled and pulled her to her feet. "Come inside. I'll make us a cup of tea and we can talk."

She stood and took hold of her crutches, and made her way into the house. He pulled out a chair for her to sit on. Just as he had the kettle under the tap to fill it, he said, "Looks like your father is heading here, to the *haus*."

Then she heard a buggy. "Really? *Ach, nee.* He asked me if I was coming to see you, and I said no. He'll never trust me now."

"You stay here. I'll see what he wants. He might not come inside."

Lucy stayed in the kitchen tracing the grain of the wooden table with her finger. If only she could hear what they were saying. All she heard were mumblings and could not make out the individual words. She drew some comfort from the fact that they weren't yelling. Although, she'd never heard either of them raise his voice in any situation.

She listened as Joshua came through the front door and then he stood, smiling in front of her. Then her *vadder* joined him.

"*Dat.* I didn't know I was going to come here. I didn't lie to you. I was at the coffee shop."

He walked toward her and sat opposite her. Joshua stayed standing. "I've made my apologies to Joshua and now I'll make them to you. I'm sorry if I made your life any less when Grace left us."

Lucy hugged her arms to her chest as she listened.

Then her father continued, "I'm sorry I called you Grace."

"*Dat*, you and *Mamm* call me Grace all the time.

Sometimes, I felt like you would've preferred I was the one to go."

He looked down. He was not a person to show his feelings or emotion of any kind.

"Grace has left us, but I'm here," Lucy said.

"I hear what you're saying, Lucy." Mr. Fuller looked at his daughter. "If you both want to continue seeing each other I won't stand in your way." He turned to Joshua. "I think you should have kept your word about marrying Grace."

Joshua looked at the floor. "I know."

"You'll be returning to the community then?" Mr. Fuller asked Joshua.

Joshua looked at him and gave a sharp nod.

Her father fixed his eyes on Lucy once more. "Joshua said he'd bring you home later." He pushed his chair out and stood up. "Not too late because your *mudder* and your *bruders* will be home tonight."

Lucy smiled. She'd missed her younger brothers and her mother, and was happy they'd cut short their visit to Ohio.

Joshua followed her father out, and not long after, Lucy heard her *vadder's* buggy horse clip-clopping away. Joshua came back into the kitchen.

Lucy raised her eyebrows. "What did he say?"

"He apologized for last night and he apologized on behalf of both sets of parents for forcing a marriage between Grace and myself."

Lucy kept quiet. Should she look surprised at the information, or tell him she'd overheard some of it the night before? Joshua sat next to her.

"I don't know if you know this, Lucy, but our parents

expected Grace and I would marry, and I was forced to go along with their plans. When I finally told Grace I didn't want to marry her, she developed the awful flu that very night."

"I thought you truly loved each other." She remembered Grace was very much in love with him.

"I loved her, but I was not in love with her enough to marry her. I know some folk think once-in-a-lifetime love doesn't exist, and others say it doesn't really matter who you marry as long as they are following *Gott's* ways. But I have never agreed with their way of thinking. I always felt in my heart, if I waited, I'd find the right woman. Do you agree?"

Lucy nodded. "What did Grace say when you ended things?"

"She was a little upset, but she understood and she said she felt the same way. She felt it was expected." He continued, "I loved Grace, but it wasn't the real, true love that one would ideally have with a woman. Yeah, we could've married and been perfectly happy like a great many folk do when they marry without love. I wanted to marry a woman who makes me miss her when I'm away from her."

Lucy's palms got sweaty. She slipped her hands under the table and wiped them on her apron. "It's not your fault Grace died."

Joshua nodded. "I know, but it makes me feel worse about putting an end to our relationship. It was bad timing. I left the community because I thought what I wanted wasn't in the community. Now, I come back here and find you. You're the part of my life that was missing." He picked up her hand.

"Now everything makes sense. You and I can live on the farm and raise *kinner* if you'll have me."

"Me?"

"Lucy, you must feel what I feel. It can't be one sided. I was sure you felt something too."

Her lips turned upward at the corners. "*Jah*, I feel it too, Joshua. It was unexpected. I didn't want to love you, thinking you and Grace had loved each other so much. But now, I feel free to have feelings for you."

"It's meant to be. Will you allow me to call on you?"

Lucy nodded. "I will." She collapsed into his arms, sobbing.

He put his arm around her back. "Hey, what is this all about? You should be happy."

She sniffed back the tears. She didn't want to be a sobbing mess in front of him. "I am happy. I didn't want to like you in that way. I tried to stop, but it was too hard." She giggled amidst the tears.

He pulled her closer. "To think I left the community in search of something that was right here all the time. I'll stay, and I'll help you persuade others to preserve the farmland for future generations."

"You will?" This was more than she'd hoped for. "You'll stay?"

He nodded then picked up her hand. "I have to; I told your *vadder* I would." He brought her hand to his lips and planted a soft kiss, sending tingles of delight through her whole body.

Lucy couldn't wait to tell the girls she and Joshua were now a couple. Not only that, but she had someone to help her in her mission to save the farmlands.

Claire was away on her honeymoon, so she'd tell her the news when she came back. They'd all be happy for her and for Joshua. Finally, she was free. Her father had apologized and she'd learned the truth about Joshua and Grace. She'd no longer be living in Grace's shadow.

Out of the five girls who'd taken jobs as maids, only Amy, their Amish deacon's daughter, was left single. It hadn't been their plan to find husbands when they'd embarked on their journey, but all the same, Lucy couldn't help but wonder what God had in store for her sweet friend Amy. She had a feeling it was something special.

* * * * *

Thank you for reading
The Amish Maid's Sweetheart.
I do hope you enjoyed it.
Samantha Price

*The next book in the Amish Maids Trilogy
is Book 3:* The Amish Deacon's Daughter.